The
Upsid
Dov
River

Tomek's
Journey

Also by Jean-Claude Mourlevat

The Upside Down River: Hannah's Journey
Jefferson

The translator would like
to thank junior language consultant
Gabriel Ardizzone.

The Upside Down River

Tomek's Journey

JEAN-CLAUDE MOURLEVAT

TRANSLATED BY ROS SCHWARTZ

ANDERSEN PRESS

First published in Great Britain in 2022 by
Andersen Press Limited
20 Vauxhall Bridge Road, London SW1V 2SA, UK
Vijverlaan 48, 3062 HL Rotterdam, Nederland
www.andersenpress.co.uk

2 4 6 8 10 9 7 5 3 1

Originally published in French in 2000 under the title *La Rivière à l'Envers:
Tomek* by Pocket Jeunesse, Département d'Univers Poche

British Library Cataloguing in Publication Data available.

ISBN 978 1 83913 198 1

Printed and bound in Great Britain by Clays Ltd, Elcograf S.p.A.

For my father

PROLOGUE

This story takes place at a time before modern comforts had been invented. There were no video games, cars with airbags or supermarkets. People didn't even have mobile phones! But there were rainbows after a shower, apricot jam with almonds, impulsive midnight dips – all the things we still enjoy nowadays. Sadly, there was also heartbreak and hay fever, against which no effective remedy has yet been found.

In other words, this all took place . . . long ago.

CHAPTER ONE

Birds of Passage

Tomek's grocery was the last house in the village. It was a tiny, simple little shop with a sign above the window saying GROCER in blue letters. When you pushed open the door, a little bell gave a cheerful *ding-ding*, and Tomek would be standing behind the counter in his grey overalls, smiling. He was quite tall for a boy of his age and rather bony, and he had a faraway look in his eyes. There would be no point trying to list all of the items Tomek sold in his shop. An entire book wouldn't be enough, whereas a single word sums it up: 'everything'. Tomek sold 'everything'. That means useful, sensible things like fly-swatters and Father Partridrigeon's cure-all elixir, but of course there were also essential items such as rubber hot-water bottles and bear knives.

Since Tomek lived in his shop, or rather in the backroom of his shop, he never closed. Although there was a little sign hanging on the door, it always showed the side that said OPEN. That didn't mean there was a continuous stream of customers. No. The villagers were respectful and took care not to bother him at all hours. But they knew that in an emergency, Tomek would willingly help them out, even in the middle of the night. And don't imagine that Tomek never left his grocery. Quite the opposite, he would often go out and stretch his legs or even take off for half a day. But then the shop would stay open and customers would go in and serve themselves. On his return, Tomek would find a note on the counter saying, '*Took a ball of sausage string, Aline*', together with the money, or, '*Came for my tobacco. Will pay tomorrow, Jack.*'

And so life was hunky-dory and things could have continued like that for years, and even centuries, without anything unusual happening.

Only, the thing is, Tomek had a secret. It wasn't anything bad, or even extraordinary, but it had crept up on him so slowly that he hadn't noticed. Exactly the way hair grows without your realising it: one day, you find it's too long, and there you are. So, one fine day, Tomek found that a thought had been growing and taking shape inside his head, and that thought was this: he was bored. Worse still, he was very bored. He had an urge to travel, to see the world.

From the little window at the back of his shop, he often used to gaze at the vast plain where the spring corn swayed gracefully, like the waves in the sea. And

4

only the *ding-ding* of the bell could tear him away from his daydreams. Other times, he would get up at dawn and go rambling along the footpaths that led deep into the countryside, through the delicate blue of the flax fields, and it was a wrench to have to go back home.

But most of all it was in autumn, when the birds of passage flew silently overhead, that Tomek felt the strongest impulse to leave. Tears came into his eyes as he watched the wild geese vanish over the horizon with a great beating of wings.

Sadly, you can't just take off and go travelling when you're called Tomek and are the owner of the only grocery in the village, the grocery that had been his father's before him and his grandfather's before *him*. What would people have thought? That he was abandoning them? That he wasn't happy among them? That he was no longer happy in the village? At any rate, they wouldn't have understood. It would have made them sad, and Tomek couldn't bear to hurt others. He resolved to stay and keep his secret to himself. I must be patient, he told himself. The boredom will eventually fade away as it came, slowly, with time, without my noticing.

Unfortunately, the exact opposite happened. In fact, an important event would soon reduce all Tomek's efforts to be reasonable to nothing.

It was a late summer's evening and Tomek had left his shop door open to enjoy the coolness of the night.

He was busy doing his accounts in his special ledger, by the light of an oil lamp, pensively chewing the end of his pencil, when a clear voice almost made him jump: 'Do you sell barley sugars?'

He looked up and saw the loveliest person you can imagine. She was a girl of around twelve, with very dark hair, wearing sandals and a dress in a pitiful state. A leather waterskin dangled from her belt. She had come in through the open door so silently that she could have been an apparition, and now she was gazing at Tomek with her sad, dark eyes: 'Do you sell barley sugars?'

Tomek did two things at the same time. The first was to answer: 'Yes, I sell barley sugars.'

And the second thing that Tomek did – Tomek, who had never in his life been the least interested in girls – was to fall head over heels in love with this little scrap of a girl. It was love at first sight.

He took a barley sugar from a jar and held it out to her. She put it in her dress pocket at once but didn't seem to want to leave. She stood there gazing at the shelves and rows of little drawers that filled an entire wall.

'What have you got in all those little drawers?'

'I've got . . . everything,' replied Tomek. 'I mean all the essentials—'

'Hat elastic?'

'Yes, of course.'

Tomek climbed up his stepladder and opened a drawer right at the top: 'Here you are.'

'And playing cards?'

He came back down and opened another drawer: 'Here.'

She hesitated, and then gave a shy smile. She was clearly enjoying this: 'And pictures . . . of a kangaroo?'

Tomek had to think for a few seconds, then he hurried over to a drawer to the left: 'There you are.'

This time, the girl's dark eyes lit up and shone. It was so delightful to see her happy that Tomek's heart began to pound.

'And desert sand? Sand that's still warm?'

Tomek mounted his stepladder once more and took from a drawer a small vial of orange sand. He came down and poured the sand onto his special ledger so that the girl could touch it. She caressed it with the back of her hand then walked the tips of her nimble fingers over it.

'It's lovely and warm.'

She had moved very close to the counter, and Tomek could feel the heat of her body. Rather than touching the warm sand, he would like to have put his hand on her golden arm. She probably guessed it, adding: 'It's as warm as my arm.'

And with her free hand, she took Tomek's hand and placed it on her arm. The reflections of the oil lamp danced on her face. She left his hand there for a few seconds and then deftly moved away, twirled around then pointed at random to one of the three hundred small drawers: 'What about that one, what's in that one?'

'Oh, just thimbles,' replied Tomek, pouring the sand back into its vial through a funnel.

'And in that one?'

'Cowries . . . they're rare shells.'

'Oh,' said the girl, disappointed. 'What about that one?'

'Sequoia seeds. I can give you some as a present if you like. But don't sow them just anywhere because sequoias grow very tall.'

Tomek thought this would please her, but his words had the opposite effect. She became serious and thoughtful again. There was a renewed silence. Tomek didn't dare say anything more. A cat was standing on the threshold of the open door. It advanced gingerly, but Tomek chased it away with a sharp wave of his hand. He didn't want to be disturbed.

'So you have everything in your shop? Absolutely everything?' said the girl, looking up at him.

Tomek felt a little uncomfortable.

'Yes . . . I mean, all the essentials,' he replied with a touch of modesty.

'So,' said the timid little quavering voice, suddenly

filled with a wild hope, it seemed to Tomek, 'so perhaps you have water from the River Qjar?'

Tomek had no idea what this water was. Nor did he have any idea where this River Qjar might be. The girl realised, and a shadow clouded her gaze. She answered, without his having to ask: 'It's the water that stops people from ever dying, didn't you know?'

Tomek gently shook his head. No, he didn't know that.

'I need some,' said the girl.

Then she tapped the waterskin dangling from her belt and added: 'I'm going to find the river and put some water in here . . .'

Tomek wished she would tell him more, but she was already coming towards him and unfolding a handkerchief in which there were a few coins.

'How much do I owe you for the barley sugar?'

'One farthing,' Tomek heard himself mumble.

The girl put the coin down on the counter, turned again to look at the three hundred little drawers and flashed Tomek a parting smile.

'Goodbye.'

Then she left the shop.

'Goodbye,' stammered Tomek.

The oil lamp was growing dim. He went back and sat on his chair behind the counter. On his special ledger that was still open, lay the strange girl's coin and a few grains of orange sand.

CHAPTER TWO

Grandfather Isham

The next day and those that followed, Tomek was annoyed with himself for having accepted his visitor's money. She probably didn't have very much. Several times he found he was talking to himself. He'd say, for example: 'Nothing at all, you don't owe me anything!' or: 'Oh please, for a *barley sugar* . . .'

But no matter how many gestures of generosity Tomek could think of, it was too late. She'd paid and she had gone, leaving him to his regrets. The other thing that bothered him was the water she had talked about, and the river with a strange name which he couldn't recall. And besides, who was she, that funny girl? Where had she come from? Was she all alone? Had someone been waiting for her outside the shop? And where had she gone afterwards? Hundreds of questions with no answers . . . He tried to find out more from his customers by making discreet inquiries: 'So, what's new in the village?' Or: 'Not many people passing through here, are there?'

All in the hope that one of them would say: 'No, not many, just that young girl a few nights ago . . .'

But no one made the slightest mention of her. Tomek seemed to be the only person to have seen her. A few days went by and then, one afternoon, Tomek could stand it no longer. He couldn't bear the thought that he might never see the girl again. And not to be able to talk to anyone about her was doubly painful. And so he shut up shop, stuffed a packet of fruit pastilles in his pocket and ran as fast as he could to the other end of the village, where old Isham lived.

Old Isham was the public scribe – in other words, he wrote for people who couldn't read or write. He also read, of course. When Tomek arrived, he was in the middle of deciphering a letter for a little lady who was listening to him attentively. Tomek kept a tactful distance until they'd finished, then walked over to his friend.

'Good day, Grandfather,' he said, raising his hand to his chest.

'Good day, my son,' replied Isham, holding out both hands, palms open.

Isham was not really his grandfather and Tomek was not Isham's son, but since Isham lived alone and Tomek was an orphan, that was what they had always called each other. They were very fond of one another.

In the summer, Isham worked in a tiny, covered street stall against a wall. He sat cross-legged, surrounded by books. To join him, you had to climb three wooden steps and sit down on the floor. His customers often preferred to remain standing in the street while they dictated their letters or listened to Isham reading to them.

'Come on up, my son.'

Tomek bounded up the three steps and sat down cross-legged beside the old man.

'Are you well?' began Tomek, taking the packet of fruit pastilles from his pocket. 'Have you got plenty of work?'

'Thank you, my boy,' replied Isham, taking the sweets. 'I never have any work, as I've already told you. Never any rest either. All this is, is just life going by . . .'

Tomek found these slightly mysterious words very amusing. You could have taken Isham for a great philosopher if he weren't so greedy. He loved sweets and was capable of sulking like a three-year-old when Tomek forgot to bring him a piece of fudge, some soft nougat, a gumball or a liquorice stick. Most of all he loved little heart-shaped gingerbread biscuits, but he was happy with anything so long as it wasn't too chewy. Because of his teeth, of course.

Tomek didn't want to be away from the shop for too long, and because he was burning with curiosity, he got straight to the point: 'Tell me, Grandfather Isham, have you ever heard of the River Tchar, or Djar . . . ?'

The old man, who was already munching his fruit pastilles, pondered for a moment, then replied slowly: 'I've heard of a River . . . Qjar.'

'That's it!' exclaimed Tomek. 'Qjar! The River Qjar!'

And as he repeated it, he thought he could hear the girl saying: '. . . *water from the River Qjar*.'

'The river that flows backwards and upside down . . .' Isham went on.

'The one that . . . what?' stuttered Tomek, who had never heard of such a thing.

'That flows backwards,' Isham repeated. 'The River Qjar flows backwards.'

'Backwards? What do you mean?' said Tomek, his eyes wide.

'I mean that the water of that river flows uphill instead of down, my son. That's left you speechless, hasn't it!'

Isham burst out laughing at the expression on his young friend's face, then he took pity on him and began to explain: 'This river's source is in the ocean, do you see? Instead of flowing into the sea, it begins there. Rather as if it were sucking up the sea water. At first, it is as wide as a big river. People say that at this point, strange trees grow on its banks. Trees that stretch themselves in the morning and let out sighs in the evening. And supposedly there are species of animals that are completely unknown elsewhere.'

'What kind, for instance?' Tomek wanted to know. 'Dangerous animals?'

But old Isham shook his head. He didn't know.

'At any rate,' he went on, 'the most astonishing thing is this water that flows the wrong way—'

'But then,' broke in Tomek, who had an inquisitive mind, 'if this river, this big river, sucks up water from the sea, then the sea level should be falling . . .'

'It should, but it doesn't because of the dozens of other rivers that flow into the ocean at the same time, and in the right direction.'

'Of course,' Tomek had to admit. 'Of course.'

'Then,' Isham went on, 'the River Qjar flows up through the land. Over hundreds of miles, so they say. It becomes narrower and narrower, losing water instead of gaining it like all the world's normal rivers.'

'But where does this water disappear to?' asked Tomek. 'It must go somewhere!'

Once again, old Isham had to confess his ignorance. 'No one knows where this water goes. There are no tributaries. It's a great mystery. Have you brought me a piece of nougat?'

It took Tomek a few moments to react. He was a million miles away from thinking about nougat. He rummaged through his pockets in vain.

'No, Grandfather, but I'll bring you some later, if you want. Promise. Tell me more about this river – please!'

Old Isham, probably disappointed, muttered a few unintelligible words then continued. 'Be that as it may, the river eventually reaches the foot of a mountain called the Sacred Mountain.'

'The Sacred Mountain?' echoed Tomek, awed by the name.

'Yes. Those who have visited this mountain say that they have never seen anything so impressive. Its peaks soar above the clouds. But that doesn't deter our little river. It simply climbs *up* it. And the higher it gets, the smaller it becomes. It turns into a mountain stream, and then a little brook. All the while flowing backwards, of course, don't ever forget. And when it arrives at the very summit, it is no more than a thin trickle of water no wider than my thumb. And there it finally stops, forming a minuscule pool in the hollow of a rock, half the size of a washbasin. This water is extraordinarily pure. And it is magic, Tomek . . .'

'Magic?'

'Yes. It makes you immortal . . .'

Once again, Tomek heard the girl's clear voice: *It's the water that stops people from ever dying, didn't you know?* Isham confirmed her words.

'The only thing is,' the old man went on, 'no one has ever brought any of that water back, my boy, no one . . .'

'But surely all you'd have to do is follow this river to its source – I mean up to the top of the mountain – fill

15

a bottle with its famous water and come back down again!'

'It should be possible . . . but the fact is that no one has ever succeeded in climbing up there. And if they have, then they haven't managed to come back down again, so no one knows about it. And if someone has managed to come back down, then they have lost their supply of water on the way. And besides, there's something that makes the whole enterprise even more difficult . . .'

'What's that?'

'Well, it's that this river probably doesn't exist. Nor does the mountain.'

There was a long pause. Then old Isham eventually broke the silence: 'By the way, my boy, who told you about this river?'

Tomek suddenly remembered that his reason for coming to see his old friend had been to tell him about the girl's visit to his shop. Now he would at last be able to confide his secret and perhaps find out more.

He took a deep breath and tried to explain in detail everything that had happened that evening in his shop. He left nothing out, not the pictures of kangaroos, or the orange sand in the little vial, or the cat that tried to come in. The only detail he omitted was his hand on the girl's arm. There was no need to shout *that* from the rooftops.

Old Isham allowed him to speak until he'd finished,

then looked at him with a smile that Tomek had never seen on his face before, one that was a mixture of amusement and affection. 'Tell me, you're not in *love*, are you my boy?'

Tomek blushed to the roots of his hair. He was furious with himself and with Isham for making fun of him. Well, he could go whistle for his nougat!

He was about to leave when the old man tugged his sleeve and made him sit down again.

'Come, wait a minute . . .'

Tomek gave in. He could never stay angry with Isham for long.

'She was carrying a waterskin, did you say?'

'Yes, she was. She said that she was going to find this river water and bring some back.'

Now, Isham was no longer smiling at all.

'You see, Tomek, I don't know whether this river exists or not, but I do know that people have been looking for it for thousands of years and that no one, and I mean *no one*, has ever returned with the tiniest drop of this famous water. Entire expeditions of men in their prime, kitted out from head to foot and determined to succeed, have perished before even catching a glimpse of the Sacred Mountain. So it's all very well for your little mystery girl to tap her waterskin and say that she's going to fill it, but that's as impossible as getting corn to grow on the back of my hand.'

'So . . .' murmured Tomek after a while. 'What will happen to her?'

Isham smiled at him. 'I suggest you forget about all that, my boy. Think about something else. There are enough pretty girls in the village, aren't there? Go on, off with you. There might be some customers waiting for you . . .'

'You're probably right, Grandfather,' said Tomek, nodding his head woefully.

Then he stood up, pressed old Isham's hand and trudged slowly back to his shop.

CHAPTER THREE

Setting Off

From that day on, Tomek couldn't stop thinking about leaving. One night, he had a strange dream in which the girl was being pursued by tigers running on their two hind legs, like people. She was calling him: 'Tomek! Tomek!' He took her by the hand and the two of them ran as fast as their legs could carry them. Behind them they could hear the jaws of the men-tigers gnashing, but they managed to escape at the last minute by hiding under a rock. Tomek asked the girl how she knew his name, and she replied with a shrug: 'But everyone knows you, Tomek!' In another dream, he was leaning over the pool of pure water at the summit of the Sacred Mountain. Something was shining at the bottom of the pool, and it was the girl's coin, the one she'd used to pay for the barley sugar. He picked it up and when he turned around, she was there, smiling, dressed like a princess. And behind her, the tamed tiger-men stood guard.

Tomek decided to set off at daybreak one morning

so that no one would notice his absence straight away and so that by the time old Isham found the letter he'd left for him, he would already be far away.

In the days before his departure, he had found it hard to hide his excitement and he had the feeling people coming into the grocery were giving him strange looks. As if his grand plans were somehow visible and something was betraying him, a particular glint in his eyes, perhaps. He thought long and hard about what clothes he should take. He was in a bit of a quandary because he had no idea what lay in store for him. Would the weather be hot or cold in those distant lands? Should he take woollen socks, a thick jumper and a balaclava? Or, on the other hand, should he travel as lightly as possible so as not to weigh himself down? Nor did he know what equipment to carry. He looked for answers in some of his favourite adventure stories but couldn't find any. Most adventurers had nothing, and his hero, Robinson Crusoe, even less than the others because he'd lost everything in the shipwreck. The barley-sugar girl didn't have anything with her either, he recalled. So Tomek decided to follow their example and not to take anything with him other than the essentials.

First of all he needed a good woollen blanket, because he would probably have to sleep under the stars and the nights would quickly turn chilly.

He also needed a water bottle. Luckily, he just

happened to have one made of sealskin. He would attach it firmly to his belt and use it for himself. And also to bring back the water from the River Qjar – if he ever found it, of course.

He made himself a tiny pouch out of a piece of very strong fabric, in which he placed the girl's coin. Then he would be able to give it back to her as soon as he found her. Assuming of course that he did find her, that is . . . In the meantime, he would keep the pouch hanging around his neck on a string and tucked safely inside his shirt, and woe betide anyone who tried to take it from him.

In his trouser pockets, he put only a bear knife, in case the need arose for him to defend himself, and two handkerchiefs on which his mother had once embroidered a 'T' for Tomek.

On his last evening, after checking that everything was ready, he sat behind his counter, lit his oil lamp and wrote the following letter to Isham:

Dear Grandfather Isham,
You are always reading other people's letters but this
one is for you, and you won't have to read it out loud.
I know this is going to make you sad and I ask you to
forgive me. I left this morning to go in search of the
River Qjar. If I find it, I will bring you back some of
its water. Along the way, I hope to find the girl I told

*you about, because that's where she's heading. I'm
leaving you the key to the shop because where I'm going,
I'm likely to lose it. I'll be back as quickly as I can.
See you soon,
Love, Tomek*

He fought back his tears as he slipped the letter into the envelope. Isham had aged a lot in the past few months. His cheeks had grown hollow. His hands were like ancient parchment. Would he still be alive when Tomek returned? And besides, would he ever return? He wasn't at all certain.

He went to bed fully clothed and slept a dreamless sleep for a few hours. When he woke up, it was still dark outside, and a moonbeam feebly lit the backroom of the shop. He jumped out of bed, his heart full of joy. Today was the day! He felt as if he had waited for ever, and that the best day of his life had finally arrived. A great surge of hope ran through him. He would find the River Qjar for sure. He would climb the Sacred Mountain. He would bring back the water. He would also see the girl again and return her money to her!

He drank a big bowlful of hot chocolate and wolfed down several slices of buttered bread and jam. Then he dressed warmly, checked that the waterskin was firmly attached to his belt, that the pouch was in its place under his shirt and that he had everything he had planned to put in his pockets. At the last minute, he added a large hunk of bread. And lastly, he rolled up his woollen blanket very tightly and strapped it to his shoulders, then he went to the shop door and did something he'd never ever done before: he turned over the little sign and it now said: CLOSED.

Tomek walked through the silent streets of the village until he reached old Isham's stall. The awning was pulled down. Noiselessly he drew it aside. On Isham's writing desk, Tomek placed the key to the grocery, the envelope containing his farewell letter and a big piece of nougat.

'Goodbye, Grandfather . . .' he whispered, as if the old man could hear him. He retraced his steps and glanced at his shop one last time as he went past. Then he set out with great strides along the path he had already taken so many times. Only this time, he would not be turning back. This time, he was leaving for good. He was an adventurer. As if to greet him, a flight of geese formed a perfect V in the sky overhead. They were heading south, like Tomek. 'I'm on my way!' he yelled at them, and his chest swelled with happiness.

In those ancient times, people had a rather vague notion of geography. They believed the Earth was probably round, but many people weren't entirely convinced. 'If the Earth is round,' they said, 'do those who are underneath walk upside down? And if they don't fall off, is it because the soles of their shoes are glued to the ground?' There weren't any exact maps or signposts as there are today. People found their way with the help of the sun, the moon and the stars . . . and they very often got lost, it has to be said.

Tomek had resolved to keep heading south, where the ocean lay, according to Isham. Once there, he thought, he would have to choose whether to go right or left in search of the River Qjar. For most of the day, he travelled through familiar landscapes, from hills to plains, stopping only to eat a little of his bread, drink from his waterskin or pick some fruit from the trees.

But as evening drew near, he had the impression that the horizon was getting wider and that a never-ending, horizontal black shadow ran across it. When he was a few hundred yards away from it, he saw that it was a forest, the biggest forest he had ever seen. He wasn't too thrilled at the idea of having to walk through it, but it would probably take several days, even weeks, to walk around it . . . who knew? *Each day has enough trouble of its own*, Tomek said to himself. Now he was beginning to feel tired. So he went back a little to a spot where he had noticed a lone tree that formed a sort of umbrella and whose branches reached almost down to the ground. He squeezed under it and wrapped himself in his blanket.

Half asleep, he thought that it would be good for him to find a travelling companion, that adventurers often had one, and he would be less lonely if he did. But he was so tired that he fell asleep before he even had time to feel sad about not having anyone to share his journey.

CHAPTER FOUR

The Forest of Oblivion

When Tomek woke up, it took him a few seconds to realise that he wasn't in his own bed. But on seeing the leafy dome over him, everything came flooding back: his early-morning departure, his long trek through the countryside, the lone tree. He really *had* left. This was no dream.

A tiny blue-and-yellow bird nesting in the tree began whistling close by and it sounded like: 'Up you get, Tomek! Up you get!' He couldn't help laughing. He had the same happy feeling as the day before when he'd left the village, the same sense of freedom, the same joy. *If this is what travelling is like,* he thought, *then I want to go around the world three times!*

He was about to emerge from his hiding place when he heard strange noises outside, like the sound of paper being scrunched or perhaps twigs being piled up. Then a series of snapping sounds, as if someone was breaking some little sticks. Tomek kept absolutely still and listened carefully. After a while, he heard a huffing and puffing. There was no doubt, someone was lighting a fire. Tomek was still afraid to come out. What if this person was dangerous? Supposing they attacked him? On the other hand, if he waited for them to leave, it might be a very long time because you don't make a fire and then leave as soon as it catches. He had reached this point in his reasoning when he heard a voice. It sounded like a woman. She was humming softly:

'Little donkey, little donkey,
On the dusty road . . .'

She probably didn't know the rest of the song because she kept singing the opening words over and over again. She was busying herself, and now he could hear the clatter of pots and pans, and water being poured into them. And still the song: 'Little donkey, little donkey . . .' This person was in a cheerful mood, thought Tomek. He also concluded that a person who sang 'Little Donkey' couldn't be bad, so he poked his nose out of his hiding place.

It was indeed a woman. Strangely attired maybe, but a woman all the same. Quite short but very plump. She was wearing all sorts of mismatched clothes, in layers it seemed: a layer of darned woollen stockings, a layer of skirts, a layer of pullovers . . . She wasn't likely to feel cold. To complete the picture, on her head she wore a hat that covered both ears, and on her feet, enormous clodhoppers.

'Well, well! Hunger brings the wolf out of his lair! Do you like coffee?'

'Yes, hello, madam . . .' replied Tomek, who had never drunk coffee before.

The woman burst out laughing on seeing how shy he was.

'Oh, forget your "madam"! Call me Marie, that's fine with me, and pull up a stone by the fire if you want to sit down.'

Walking around the tree in search of a large stone, Tomek saw there was a donkey grazing, and a cart upended, its shafts pointing skywards.

'Is that your donkey?' he asked, coming back.

'That's Trotter. He's very clever. A bit stubborn but very clever. And above all, brave-hearted. Aren't you, Trotter?'

The donkey looked up, nodded his head in a strange fashion and looked at his mistress through a hairy fringe that fell over his eyes. Then he carried on munching.

'He's blind in one eye,' added the roly-poly woman. 'The bears . . .'

'Bears?' said Tomek, sitting down on a flat stone he'd found.

'Oh yes, bears. The forest is teeming with them.'

'Really . . .' said Tomek, and he gazed at the vast, silent, motionless black shadow.

He realised that he had almost forgotten it.

'So it's not possible to cross it?'

The woman, who was cutting a slice from a huge rye loaf, stopped with the knife in mid-air.

'You want to cross the forest?'

'Yes,' replied Tomek, and he had the impression he'd made a blunder.

To correct it, he added at once: 'Or, if it's not possible, I'll go around the edge . . .'

'You'll go around the edge,' echoed the woman, and she burst into such a cheerful, natural laugh that Tomek began to laugh too.

They laughed until they cried, especially as Tomek hammed it up by repeating every so often, 'I'll go around the edge . . .' and the woman guffawed even louder, echoing, as if it was a completely natural thing to do, 'Of course, you'll go around the *edge*!'

Once they'd calmed down, Marie went over to the cart and brought back a basket containing a pound of butter, two jars of jam, one strawberry and the other blackberry, a large hunk of ewe's milk cheese, cow's milk in a little churn and a tin of sugar. Meanwhile, the coffee in the saucepan was lovely and hot. She poured some into a cup for Tomek and nudged the basket of food towards him, inviting him to tuck in. They ate in silence and heartily. Then Marie rolled a cigarette and began to smoke it, which amazed Tomek as he had never seen a woman do that.

'What's your name, by the way?' Marie asked eventually, blowing out the smoke.

'Tomek. I'm Tomek.'

'Well, Tomek, you need to know that to walk around this forest, to "go around the edge," ' – and they nearly started laughing again – 'to go all the way around it would probably take more than two years.'

'Two years!' repeated Tomek, shocked.

'Yes, that forest is the mother of all forests, it's the oldest and the biggest. At any rate, the broadest. Do you know what it's called?'

'No,' replied Tomek.

'It's called . . . Trotter!'

For a moment, Tomek thought the forest was called Trotter, and he considered that an ill-chosen name for such a formidable forest, but no, Marie had simply broken off to call her donkey.

'Trotter! Do you want a piece of cheese for your dessert?'

The donkey shook his tail, which probably meant yes, because Marie got up to take it to him.

'It's called the Forest of Oblivion. And do you know why?'

'No,' replied Tomek, thinking to himself that he really didn't know very much.

'It's called the Forest of Oblivion because those who enter it are immediately forgotten . . .'

'You mean they don't ever come back and people forget they ever lived?'

'No. Not at all. I mean that people forget them the minute they enter. As if they didn't exist any more, as if they had *never* existed. The forest swallows them whole, and with them people's memories of them. They are both out of sight and out of mind. Do you understand?'

'Not exactly . . .'

'Right. I'm going to give you an example. Your parents are probably thinking about you right now, they'll be wondering where you are, what you—'

Tomek broke in: 'I don't have any parents. I'm an orphan.'

'All right, then give me the name of someone who knows you very well and who loves you very much.'

Tomek answered without hesitation: 'Isham. He's my best friend.'

'Perfect. This person is very likely thinking about you right now, wondering if you're all right, what you're doing and when you'll be coming back, isn't he?'

'Yes, I'm sure he is . . .' replied Tomek, and he felt a pang.

'Well as soon as you set foot in this forest, Esham—'

'*I*-sham,' Tomek corrected her.

'*Isham* won't have the slightest recollection of you. For him, you will never have existed, and if anyone asks him for news of Tomek, which is impossible in fact, because no one can ask for news of a person who no longer exists – but let's suppose they could – and so they ask for news of Tomek, well, he'll answer, "News of who?", and that's how it will be for as long as you stay in the forest. But then, as soon as you come out again, everything will be as it was before, and your friend Isham might be thinking, "I wonder what that rascal Tomek is up to right now?"'

'And . . . and supposing I don't get out?' asked Tomek weakly.

'If you don't get out, then you'll be forgotten for all time. Your name won't mean anything to anyone. It will be as if you hadn't ever lived.'

Never could Tomek have imagined such a terrible thing. He ate up his slice of bread and butter and drank his coffee in silence, while Marie finished her cigarette, and all of a sudden, he had a crazy idea.

'So, Marie, if you were to go into the forest right now, but only a few feet in, does that mean you'd no longer exist for me?'

'Exactly, Tomek. Would that be fun to try?'

'Fun' wasn't quite the right word. It even sounded a

little scary, but he agreed anyway, and they both hurriedly cleared away the remains of the breakfast and put out the fire. Then Marie hitched the cart to Trotter as if he were a real little pony. They jumped in and she shouted: 'Giddy up, Trotter!'

The donkey began to trot in the direction of the forest, and they reached it within a few minutes. Tomek kept asking himself whether he really wanted to take part in this strange experiment, but Marie was already shoving him out of the cart.

'Right, I'm going to go a little way into the forest with Trotter. I'll stay there for around three minutes, then I'll come back out. I only hope you won't have the bright idea of going into the forest yourself, or we'll never find each other. Or rather find ourselves! How old are you, Tomek?'

'I'm thirteen.'

'That's all right then. No thirteen-year-old would dare enter this forest alone. See you later, Tomek! Giddy up, Trotter!'

The donkey set off, pulling the cart. Marie gave one last wave and vanished between the black tree trunks of the Forest of Oblivion.

Tomek took a few steps back to get a better view of the impressive wall of trees that rose up before him. It was made up of a species of very dark, very dense pine trees, at least two hundred and fifty feet high. Without even entering the forest, you could feel its coolness. *It must be very dark in there*, Tomek thought anxiously. Perhaps it was more reasonable to bypass this forest and walk around the edge. At this thought, he had a curious urge to laugh, even though it wasn't funny. There was nothing exciting about the idea of losing several days or even weeks . . . If only he'd had a travel companion with him, of course, he would have seen things differently. When there are two of you, you encourage one another, you egg each other on, you can laugh together and help one another if necessary. But since his departure, he hadn't met anyone. And he'd ended up sleeping under that tree back there, all alone, wrapped in his blanket. His blanket! He'd forgotten his *blanket*!

He ran back to the tree as fast as his legs could carry him and dived between its branches. Phew! It was still there. He promised himself to be more careful in future. An adventurer mustn't lose his belongings, especially when he has so few. It was only when he emerged from his hiding place that he saw the remains of a fire close to the tree. And yet he could have sworn that there had been nothing there the previous day when he'd arrived. And no one had come since. That was very odd.

He rolled up the blanket and strapped it to his shoulders and took a few steps in the direction of the forest. Maybe it wasn't as big as all that, after all. If he left straight away and walked fast, he might get through it by midday, or at least by nightfall, and if he came across any wild bears, he had his bear knife in his pocket.

Before entering the forest, he hesitated one last time, because it occurred to him that he hadn't eaten any breakfast and that he'd probably need all his energy. But he was surprised to note that he wasn't hungry, and that he even felt completely full. *Go on, Tomek!* he urged, and he advanced towards the forest with a determined step.

He was about to enter it when he heard branches snapping close by. Was that an animal? A human being? The noise was getting closer. Tomek hastily retreated and lay down in the tall grass to see what would appear out of the gloom. What he saw first of all was two donkey ears, then a donkey's head, then an entire donkey, and lastly a cart pulled by the donkey and, on the cart, a plump, smiling woman. Relieved, he stood up.

'So, Tomek! Has your memory come back?' shouted Marie cheerfully.

Tomek raced over to the cart. Marie had stepped down and was holding out her arms. Tomek felt awkward letting her hug him because he didn't know her well enough yet. So he simply took her hands and squeezed them. That was how they became friends.

CHAPTER FIVE

Marie

At first, the forest wasn't at all as dense or dark as Tomek had feared. Quite the opposite, the light filtered through the branches and cascaded onto the ground strewn with pine needles. A very clear path led straight ahead, and the carpet of moss was so thick that you could barely hear Trotter's hooves. The little donkey clip-clopped along happily, effortlessly pulling the cart on which Marie and Tomek were sitting. For the time being, there was nothing to fear from bears because, according to Marie, their territory was more than five hours away and there would be plenty of time to worry about them later. They chatted away easily, as happens when two people who barely know one another hit it off immediately. Tomek learned that Marie was in the habit of sleeping under the lone tree and had been surprised the previous evening to find someone there. But he was asleep so soundly that she hadn't had the heart to wake him and had spent the rest of the night in her cart. He also learned that she only went through the forest once a year. It was pure chance that it was today, the same day as Tomek. When he asked her why she made this journey, she hesitated and then asked, 'Are you really interested?'

'Yes,' replied Tomek, 'and if you like, afterwards I'll tell you why I want to go through the forest too.'

'Very well, my dear. After all, it's not often I have the opportunity to tell my tale and I'd like to. But make yourself comfortable because it's a long one.'

Tomek, who loved stories, snuggled under his blanket, for the air had grown cooler, and waited.

Marie rolled herself another cigarette, slipped on an extra jacket and then began: 'My dear Tomek, you might find it hard to believe, and I wouldn't be offended – nothing offends me any more these days – you might find it hard to believe that at eighteen, I was a pretty girl. A very pretty girl, even. And on top of that, my father was one of the wealthiest shopkeepers in our town, so you can imagine that men were queuing up to marry me. Have you ever seen bees buzzing around a teaspoonful of jam? Well that's what the boys were like around me. All of them. Except that I was in no hurry to get married. It was so funny watching them filing past beneath our windows. There were all kinds: small, fat, ugly, almost handsome, hideous, deformed, almost upright, bow-legged, every type, you name it. What fun my sisters and I had watching them! We giggled ourselves silly behind the curtains. A few years went by and then my sisters got married and I wanted to be like them. So I chose the fellow who seemed like the best match. He was good-looking, Tomek, really good-looking, I assure you. Slim, with a handsome face and noble features. Very clever, too: everyone agreed it was a pleasure to listen to him talk. And he also had property. In short, when I add that he was tremendously kind and attentive to my slightest wish, you will understand that I'd found that rare bird, as they say! The wedding took place two months later. It was a madly joyous event. Everyone was happy on that day, I think. Most of all me. But, you see, Tomek, then the following happened—Whoa there, Trotter!'

The donkey was going faster and faster and was almost galloping, which made the cart lurch dangerously. But he obeyed his mistress's order at once and slowed down to a gentle trot.

'Yes, the following happened. Not three days had gone by when I realised there was a little problem: the thing was, I didn't *love* him . . .'

'You . . . you didn't love him?' said Tomek, wide-eyed.

'No, I didn't love him,' replied Marie, and she began to chortle, and Tomek soon joined in.

'But you mean . . . not at all?'

'Not the tiniest bit!'

And the pair of them split their sides laughing again.

Wiping away his tears, Tomek thought, *This woman's definitely a real character!*

After a few minutes, once she'd stopped laughing, Marie was able to carry on with her story and she continued: 'Separation was out of the question. It wasn't done. Just think what a scandal it would have caused if I'd admitted the truth! No one had forced me, after all. I only had myself to blame. I'd chosen that young man on my own! But the thing is, I didn't know what I was doing, you *don't* know what you're doing at twenty, and I'd forgotten that to appeal to me, a person had to be fun. Because I happen to enjoy laughing, as you've probably noticed. And the thing is, he was no fun . . . but I didn't realise it until too late. I spent a few miserable days. I knew that my life would be ruined if I didn't do something. So one night – we'd been married for less than a week – I crept out of bed, put on the first coat and pair of shoes I laid my hands on and slipped out into the street. I went and knocked on the windowpane of a lowly barrow boy called Barnaby who I'd known for ages. I always bought fruit from his cart at the market. He was a little in love with me, it was obvious. I was fond of him because he was kind, and fun. He opened the window and I asked him: "Will you take me away?"

'He said: "Where to?"

'I said: "Wherever you like. Far from here!"

'He didn't even ask when we'd be coming back, or if

we'd be coming back at all. Two minutes later, he'd hitched his cart to his donkey and thrown in a few clothes grabbed at random. We jumped in and left the town. Well, just think, I knew at once that I would always love this man, just as I had known that I'd never love the other one . . . You see how sometimes in life the most serious problems sometimes work themselves out . . . In short, the little donkey trotted all through the rest of the night. I recall that at one point I was about to start crying because I realised that I'd left without even saying goodbye to my sisters, and that's when the donkey began to fart. Barnaby said: "Excuse him, he's a farter." But the donkey carried on, and the more we laughed, the more he farted. It could have been a very romantic moment: the two lovers eloping, the starry sky and all that, but that donkey had to be a farter! As a matter of fact, Trotter here is the grandson of that infamous donkey and he is absolutely worthy of his grandfather, as you will certainly have the opportunity to hear very soon. Barnaby and I spent years living on the road, selling fruit and vegetables. To avoid being recognised, I allowed myself to put on a few pounds. After spending my life trying to lose weight, I found it very enjoyable to do the opposite. Barnaby didn't mind, he'd call me "My little pudding!" and shower me with kisses! Oh, we weren't rolling in money, far from it, but if only you knew how we laughed. It was the happiest time of my life. And then, one fine day, we learned that horsemen were after us, that we were still wanted. We'd heard about this Forest of Oblivion and we thought that it was exactly what we needed. People would forget us, and that way we'd be left in peace. That was all we asked for, just to be left in peace . . .'

At this point in Marie's story, Tomek shuddered. All of a sudden, he recalled where he was and what that meant: right now he didn't exist for anyone except this jolly lady who he'd only met a few hours ago and who was telling him her life story. He forced himself to listen to the rest of her tale so as not to fret too much.

'We came to the spot where I met you yesterday,' Marie went on, 'and we didn't hesitate for long. Barnaby said, "Giddy up, Trotter!". (That donkey was called Trotter. All three were called Trotter: the grandfather, the father and the son. All three of them farters.) So, we entered the forest. For me, it was the first time. As it is for you, today. I'll spare you the details of our journey through it, otherwise we'll still be on the same subject tomorrow. Besides, you'll be able to find out about it all for yourself. Anyhow, once we came out the other side, we wondered whether we were dreaming. Imagine a sea of flowers, as far as the eye can see, flowers of every colour, shape and size. An avalanche of fragrances. Barnaby was behaving as if he was drunk, rushing about in all directions. He plucked a big purple flower and put it on his head like a hat, yelling, "Captain Barnaby at your service!" I was over the moon with excitement too. I burst out laughing and shouted, "At ease, captain!" Then he keeled over backwards, stiff as a poker, to make me laugh, of course, and lay there absolutely still. I ran over to kiss him, and that's when I saw he was dead. His head had hit the only rock in the meadow. The only one, I swear to you. I called to him, "Barnaby! Barnaby!" but he didn't answer. He was smiling at me with his funny hat on his head. A person couldn't die happier. I was about to burst into tears when Trotter let out a loud volley of farts. So, in a trice – you see I've always made my decisions in a trice – I decided that I wouldn't cry, that I would never cry again, but on the contrary, I'd carry on celebrating life as I'd done before, with Barnaby. I dug a hole and laid him in it. There was no lack of flowers to decorate the grave! And then I simply said I'd come back to see him the following year, that I'd come back to see him *every* year. And that's what I've done ever since . . . There, that's my story, Tomek. But, hey, you're not going to start crying, are you?!'

Tomek was trying to keep his lip from trembling. But she was the one who'd been through all that, and if she wasn't crying, he wasn't going to cry when he'd merely listened to her. He gritted his teeth, then asked, 'And after that you came back to this side of the forest? But it must have been nice there, with all those flowers.'

'Of course I thought about staying there, especially as I knew they were looking for me on this side. Then Trotter and I set off across this vast meadowland. But do you know what? It's impossible to travel more than half a mile.'

'Why's that?' asked Tomek.

'Simply because the scents drive you crazy. They go to your head and you start hallucinating. You become delirious. It's very nice and very funny, but you'd probably die if you went on. Luckily, Trotter was more resistant than me. I just had the presence of mind to say, "Turn around, Trotter!" before passing out, and he brought me back to Barnaby's grave, at the edge of the forest, where the fragrances were less overpowering. And we crossed it in the other direction.'

A long silence followed Marie's story. Trotter Junior trotted steadfastly. Tomek became aware that it was much darker than earlier and that the air was a lot chillier.

'What about you?' said Marie. 'What brings you here? Your turn to tell your story now.'

'Yes,' replied Tomek pulling his blanket tighter around him, 'but my story isn't as interesting as yours. It so happened that I wanted very much to go travelling. I have a little grocery in my village, and I think I was a little bored. And I'm looking for the River Qjar. Do you know it?'

Marie had never heard of it.

'It's a river that flows backwards and upside down, so they say, and if you succeed in following it all the way to the end, at the summit of a mountain called the Sacred Mountain, well, you can scoop up some of its water, which is said to stop people from ever dying.'

'Really?' exclaimed Marie. 'And who told you about this river?'

'My friend Isham. He's very old now and I'd very much like to take him some of this water.'

'You are a very brave boy, Tomek,' said Marie after a silence. 'Tell me, when I came out of the forest during our experiment earlier, were you not about to enter it?'

'I think I was,' replied Tomek, rather proud of himself.

'So you want to find this water for your friend Isham and that's what made you leave your home.'

'Yes, that's right.'

'No other reason?' asked Marie.

'No other reason,' replied Tomek.

He vaguely felt that there was something else, but he couldn't quite put his finger on it. He racked his brains trying to recall it, but in vain.

Then they stopped talking and allowed themselves to be lulled by the regular swaying of the cart as it trundled along the track.

CHAPTER SIX

Bears

After they'd been travelling for an hour, long enough for Tomek to realise that Marie hadn't exaggerated Trotter's musical prowess, darkness fell and they could barely see. What's more, a damp cold had engulfed the cart and its passengers.

'Whoa, Trotter!' shouted Marie, and the donkey stopped dead.

Then she handed the shivering Tomek a jacket.

'Here, put this on. It will get even colder shortly. And I'm going to put our little friend's slippers on him.'

Tomek wondered what that meant, and he watched her. She rummaged around in the cart and extracted an armful of fabrics which she threw onto the ground. Then she clambered down and began to wrap each of Trotter's hooves, so he ended up with a sort of big ball around each foot. Tomek didn't understand.

'There we are. And now the wheels! I need your help, Tomek!'

He jumped down from the cart and they did the same to the wheels as Marie had done to Trotter's hooves: they twisted long ribbons of fabric around them which they then tied to the spokes. The cart now had proper tyres! Tomek was about to ask Marie what the point of all that was, when they heard a shrill cry, followed immediately by a terrible growling that made the forest tremble. It was more like a howl of pain than that of an animal attacking. Trotter froze. Marie and Tomek strained their ears, but the forest had fallen silent again.

'What was that?' asked Tomek, clutching Marie's arm.

'I don't know,' she admitted. 'A bear, for certain. Who must have injured himself very badly. But the scream beforehand? I don't know . . . It sounded like . . . No, I don't know . . .'

Then, since they heard nothing more, they climbed back onto the cart and set off again. To Tomek's great surprise, the donkey and cart were now almost silent. You could barely hear the clip-clop of Trotter's hooves, or the even the faintest rumble from the wheels. It felt as if they were gliding.

'And now I'm going to explain,' whispered Marie.

'Please do,' replied Tomek, 'because I give in.'

'Well the thing is,' Marie went on, 'as I've already told you, this forest is teeming with bears. Their territory only begins here, which is why we haven't seen any yet.

They're a very degenerate species of bear, because they're the only living creatures in this forest and, as you probably know, inbreeding causes defects. On top of that, as a result of living in the dark, they've become completely blind. Their sense of smell isn't very good either, they wouldn't be able to tell the difference between a roast chicken and a wild strawberry. Their only sharp sense is their hearing. They have a good ear and spend their time listening out for the slightest sound. They're tired of eating tasteless mushrooms and mouldy moss, and for them, a noise means meat, do you see? They themselves are very quiet, despite their bulk. They move silently and suddenly appear in front of you. To them, we are meat, Tomek, don't forget that for one moment during the next two or three hours. Don't speak. Don't move. Don't breathe noisily and above all, for the love of God, don't sneeze! This forest is probably full of dead brave souls devoured by the bears because they sneezed or simply cleared their throats.'

'But ... what about Trotter?' whispered Tomek, terrified. 'Supposing he ... I mean, what if he starts to—'

'Trotter is cleverer than you think. He's already lost an eye in this forest and he knows that his survival depends on keeping quiet. He'll be able to control himself. Oh, yes, one last thing: these bears are ... how can I put it ... they're big.'

'Very big?' asked Tomek.

'Very big,' confirmed Marie. 'And now, silence. Not a peep until I give you the signal.'

They continued gliding through the dark. Tomek could barely make out the hindquarters of Trotter, who was prancing ahead of him. Despite Marie's comforting words, he only felt half confident. He said a quick prayer that began with: 'Dear Lord, let me see the light of day again, let me see Grandfather Isham again . . .' and that ended with: 'I beg you, Trotter, please don't fart!'

It is hard to gauge the time when everything around you is dark and silent. Had one hour gone by, or maybe two? Had he dozed off? In any case, Tomek suddenly had the feeling that they were standing still. Trotter had stopped. What could that mean? He was careful not to even bat an eyelid. What was Marie doing? Why was she not moving either? Was she asleep? And why wasn't Trotter setting off again? Tomek soon had the answer to all these questions. A feeble ray of sunlight filtered through the high branches, falling just in front of the donkey. And there, bang in the middle of the track, sat a bear. Tomek felt chilled to the bone, but he managed not to cry out. Never in his life had he seen such a huge creature. The bear was absolutely motionless, except for its enormous head which sometimes swivelled or gave a slight nod, and the small, hairy ears which slowly pivoted, alert to the faintest rustle among the leaves, the tiniest stone rolling. As Marie had said: the bear couldn't see anything, couldn't smell anything, but it was listening. Oh, how it was listening! It was all ears. It listened so intently that Tomek was afraid it would hear his heart thumping wildly in his chest. He remembered having seen a bear once, in the market square in his village. The handler made it dance to the sound of his flute, but this one was much bigger and much more powerful.

The wait went on for ages. Trotter was as still as a stone statue. Marie gave no sign of life either. Tomek resolved to be patient too, even if this were to last for days and nights. The bear would have to go away eventually! In the position he was lying, Tomek would be able to hold on for a long time. They'd see whose patience ran out first! But there was something around his neck that was bothering him. It felt like a string. He raised his hand inch by inch, taking infinite care. It was indeed a string. He slid it gently through his fingers to find out what could be on the end of it, and he found a sort of small hessian pouch tied with a drawstring. Taking his time, he managed to undo the knot. The pouch contained a coin which just fitted inside. Tomek turned it over and over in his hand. A farthing, he reckoned. It was warm from having lain against his chest. Why had he put it there? He had no recollection . . .

Time went by, impossible to tell how long. At one point he gave a slight shudder. He had almost fallen asleep. But he mustn't, no matter what happened. When you're asleep, you might snore, or move. There's nothing noisier than a person sleeping! Was it Tomek's shudder that had alerted the bear? Whatever it was, the animal was on the move. It placed its two forepaws on the ground and started ambling. Luckily, it wasn't heading towards the cart. On the contrary, it was walking away.

Just then, Tomek heard Marie's voice whispering in his ear. She murmured, 'They're going . . .'

They? pondered Tomek. How come 'they'? There was only one, wasn't there? He wanted to look behind him, but Marie stopped him. They had to be patient a little longer before moving even a little finger. So they waited a few more minutes, then Tomek was allowed to turn around. He thought he would faint with terror. The bear that was lumbering off into the darkness must have been more than thirty-five feet tall. A mountain of flesh, claws and teeth who, with a single swipe, could have destroyed the cart and its occupants. When Marie judged that they were completely out of danger, she murmured, 'Giddy up, Trotter!'

And the little donkey set off again, as silent as a fly on a velvet carpet.

Soon, they were able to converse again in hushed voices.

'The one in front of the cart was a baby,' said Marie. 'He was only a few months old, no more. The other one was the mother, I think.'

'Luckily I didn't see her,' replied Tomek, 'otherwise I'd never have been able to stop myself from screaming.'

He pulled his blanket up under his chin and breathed deeply. Had it not been for Marie and Trotter, he wouldn't have had the slightest chance of surviving. He'd have ended up as a bear's dinner, forgotten by everyone for ever. He shuddered at the thought. To think that the barley-sugar girl had had to face that too, that she'd had to confront those fearsome bears all on her own, to *think* . . . Tomek suddenly froze with horror. The scream they'd heard a few hours earlier! It had been her! It could only have been her! On the verge of tears, he cried out: 'Marie, Marie, she's been gobbled up! She—'

'Stop shouting, for goodness' sake!' Marie interrupted him. 'Who's been gobbled up?'

'The girl! That was her screaming, I'm certain of it! Marie, we have to do something!'

'Who on earth are you talking about, Tomek? What girl?'

He realised he hadn't told Marie about her yet. Strangely, it hadn't occurred to him, and yet God knows he thought about her all the time. He also remembered with a jolt that earlier he'd been puzzled by the coin he'd found in the tiny pouch around his neck. He told Marie, who mulled it over for a few seconds then said, 'Well if you'd forgotten her, Tomek, that can only mean one thing, which is—'

Tomek finished Marie's sentence for her glumly. '. . . that *she* was in the Forest of Oblivion . . . so it was definitely her screaming. And so it was her who the bears . . .'

He tailed off. He pictured her, so pretty in the soft glow of the oil lamp: '*Do you sell barley sugars?*'

What was the point of going on with his journey now? What was the point of going on living, even? He felt like shouting at the top of his voice: 'You don't scare me, you big, stupid bears!'

He wanted to sing his lungs out and bang saucepans to attract them, so they would gobble him up too and that would be the end of it. The only thing stopping him was Marie and Trotter, because unlike him, they didn't want to die. He hid under the blanket to cry. They ploughed on for a long time like that. Tomek was heartbroken. Marie had placed her hand on his shoulder and from time to time she stroked him as if to say, 'It's all right . . . everything's going to be all right . . .' Then suddenly she hugged him tighter and murmured, 'Tomek! I've been thinking: there's something that didn't occur to either of us.'

'What's that?' he sniffed.

'If you didn't remember your girlfriend earlier, it's because she was in the Forest of Oblivion, right?'

'Yes, so what?'

'And now you can remember her ... She's come back into your memory ...'

Tomek, who was gradually beginning to grasp what Marie meant, threw off his blanket.

'Yes, but of course! If I'm thinking of her again, it means she's not in the Forest of Oblivion any more ... She got out! Marie! She got out!'

They hugged each other for joy. Trotter speeded up and soon the three of them reached the edge of the bears' territory. They could speak in their normal voices again, see better and above all feel a little warmth on their skins. As the miles flew by, delighted to be back in daylight, Tomek and Marie began to sing all the songs that came into their heads and they ended up yelling at the tops of their voices:

'Little donkey, little donkey
On the dusty road!'

Trotter, infected by their good spirits, galloped like a young donkey, and soon they emerged into the light of the meadow, leaving behind them the Forest of Oblivion and its gloom.

CHAPTER SEVEN

The Meadow

Barnaby's grave was very simple. A small earth mound on which Marie had placed a cross made of two hazelnut branches. White flowers had sprung up over it, making it the most charming little tomb, as cheerful most likely as Barnaby had been in his life. Tomek and Marie contemplated it for a moment in silence, then Marie said affectionately: 'At ease, captain . . .'

Her eyes were bright, but she didn't cry.

The meadow was more beautiful than anything Tomek had ever seen. Imagine a garden where only flowers grew: purple, white, red, yellow, blooms as black as night, each more dazzling than the one before.

Well, spread out before Tomek were a million gardens like that one, as far as the eye could see.

He took a few steps forward into the meadow and bent over the first flowers. They were like pansies with their velvet petals, but they were as green as if freshly painted. He picked one and raised it to his nostrils.

It smelled like a mixture of pepper and chocolate. It wasn't unpleasant. He breathed in again, deeply, and suddenly he noticed that on his hands he was wearing his thick winter mittens, the ones he'd had when he was a little boy. He'd lost them one day and had never found them again. It made him hoot with laughter and he wanted to show them to Marie.

'Marie, Marie, come and see! Look at my hands! I've found my old winter mittens! The ones I had when I was little!'

She came running over and slapped Tomek's wrist to make him drop the flower.

'Keep away from this flower, Tomek! And I forbid you to pick any more!'

Then she dragged him over to the entrance to the woods, where Trotter was waiting patiently for them.

'Tomek, these are unknown species. Better safe than sorry.'

Then they went to look for dry wood in the forest. When they came out, Trotter was braying pitifully. For a few moments, the poor creature had thought he'd been abandoned. On spotting his two friends, he jumped with delight and let out a volley of joyous toots to greet them.

They made a fire and Marie cooked a big potful of potatoes with bacon. Then they ate their meal with gusto as they watched the sun set over the meadow. Finally, as night was falling, they arranged two makeshift beds in the cart and lay down, side by side.

'Good night, Tomek,' said Marie. 'I'm glad I met you. Glad to have been able to talk to you about Barnaby.'

'Good night, Marie,' stuttered Tomek, and he fell into a peaceful sleep.

The following morning, while they were having breakfast, Marie told Tomek that she was going to spend the day beside Barnaby and that she'd be back that evening. What about him, what were his plans?

'I think,' replied Tomek, 'that I'm going to try and cross the meadow. I'll pinch my nose and it'll be fine!'

'I knew it!' said Marie. 'When I saw you were prepared to risk going through the forest on your own, I knew you were capable of anything!'

She didn't try to dissuade him. She made him a bundle to carry on his shoulder, as well as the blanket, and she filled it with provisions: bread, of course, and also cheese, nuts and biscuits. And lastly, Tomek poured cold water into his waterskin and bunged up his nose with two little plugs of fabric he'd fashioned. He tested them by smelling the remains of the coffee and then one of the green flowers. The result was conclusive: he couldn't smell anything but he could breathe freely.

Finally, it was time to say farewell.

'If you change your mind, or if something goes

wrong,' said Marie, 'you'll have until this evening to turn back and find me here. And now, go! I don't like goodbyes and neither does Trotter!'

They hugged, and with a heavy heart, Tomek set off across the meadow.

'Goodbye, Marie! Goodbye, Trotter!' he called.

'Goodbye, Tomek,' replied Marie, laughing warmly. 'And don't forget: I'll be back here in exactly one year. Perhaps we'll meet again!'

'Perhaps!' echoed Tomek, and he did not look back.

The little fabric noseplugs worked perfectly, and Tomek walked for most of the day without being affected by the flowers' fragrance. He kept up a good pace. The barley-sugar girl had not been far ahead of them in the forest, he told himself. She had only emerged a few hours before them, and even if she hadn't slept for an entire night as they had, she couldn't be very far ahead. Of course, the forest was vast and perhaps she'd taken a path miles and miles away from the one they'd followed. How could he know?

Every second, Tomek discovered new kinds of flowers. He didn't recognise any of them. Now he was walking through a sea of yellow, amid giant tulips heavy with a golden powder which blew into the air at the slightest puff of wind. Now it was a symphony of reds and tiny florets that all merged into one big scarlet carpet on which you walked without a sound. The most splendid were giant blue flowers whose petals, as big as bedsheets, floated like aquatic plants on a seabed.

As the afternoon was drawing to a close, he stopped for a little rest, and, to his great surprise, he realised he was carrying a bundle on his shoulder, as well as his blanket. He opened it and found food: bread, of course, and also cheese, nuts and biscuits. He didn't recall bringing it. So there could only be one explanation: the person who had given him these provisions was now in the Forest of Oblivion. That was why he had no recollection of anyone giving it to him. Was it a man? A woman? Several people or only one? He didn't have the faintest idea. At any rate, he thought, taking a bite of the cheese, it's someone who's very fond of me, otherwise they wouldn't have given me all this . . .

Then he set off again and walked on for a long time, without feeling tired, his heart lighter. He began to hum, '*Little donkey, little donkey, on the dusty road,*' when he suddenly sensed that someone was following him. He turned around and saw a young calf trotting behind him. He rubbed his eyes but when he looked again, the little creature had vanished.

But something else happened: Tomek's hair had now rapidly grown down to below his waist. He grabbed the pair of scissors kindly held out to him by a giant hen in a business suit who was walking alongside him, and started to cut it, but the more he chopped, the faster his hair grew.

'*Chop, chop! Chop, chop!*' sang a choir of potbellied little men, their hands clasped over their paunches. Tomek burst out laughing. Then all these characters – the young calf (who had come back), the rotund choristers and the hen in a business suit – were walking in step and singing louder than ever:

> '*Chop, chop,*
> *Choppity chop,*
> *Chop, chop,*
> *Choppity chop,*
> *Chop, chop, chop!*

Tomek almost fell over from laughing. But as they were all bellowing with gusto, he joined in, singing louder and louder:

> '*Chop, chop,*
> *Choppity chop,*
> *Chop, chop,*
> *Choppity chop,*
> *Chop, chop, chop!*

> *Turkeys go gobble gobble,*
> *Ducks go waddle waddle,*

Squirrels have bushy tails,
And snails leave slimy trails.

Soon they had to stop because they were laughing so hard, but also to allow a caravan of miniature dromedaries coming from the right to cross. Then came three sets of twins carrying a seventh boy in a jute sack. They were all heading westwards.

'Hello, boys!' shouted Tomek, merrily.

They didn't reply, and the last one even looked daggers at him, as if to say, 'D'you want to paint my portrait?'

This sobered Tomek a little. He was suddenly overcome with exhaustion. He sat down, but that wasn't enough, and eventually he stretched out on the ground. His head lay on a cushion of purple flowers whose scent reminded him of his feather pillow.

The *scent*? He shouldn't have been able to smell anything because of the little fabric bungs in his nose. He raised his hand to check and found they'd gone! They must have fallen out without him noticing . . . He realised that he must quickly make two more, but it was too late, he was already falling asleep.

Three field mice dressed in white lab coats and wearing rimmed spectacles came and sat on a bench a few inches from his face. They observed him closely, frowning, then one spoke: 'He needs a pillow! Bring him a pillow!'

'Definitely,' said another. 'To sleep well, you need a pillow.'

'No . . . thank you . . . I . . . I don't need a . . . pi . . .' stammered Tomek, overcome by drowsiness. 'I . . . I don't want to sleep . . . It's . . . it's . . . dangerous . . . I mustn't . . . I mustn't . . .'

'Of course you must!' said the third mouse. 'What better than a little snooze when you're tired? Bring him a pillow!'

Tomek felt his head being raised and his own pillow being slipped under it, his feather pillow. His eyelids were closing but he could still see the three mice smiling at him.

'There,' said the first mouse. 'That's good.'

'No . . . it's not . . . it's not good . . .' said Tomek with his little remaining energy. 'You . . . you are . . . field mice . . . Mice . . . can't . . . can't talk. I want . . . I want to go . . . home . . .'

'Of course,' said the second mouse.

'Absolutely,' said the third.

And Tomek felt himself slipping, slipping, without being able to stop himself. He was falling into the abyss. He wanted to say something else, but the words no longer came out of his mouth. Instead, they clanged like bells inside his head. Then the bells stopped their racket and there was nothing.

CHAPTER EIGHT

The Awakening Words

'Under . . . the . . . belly . . . of the cocro . . . of the crocro . . . of the cro-co-dile . . .' said the tiny voice.

Tomek woke up and half opened his eyes. He found himself in a perfectly tidy room that smelled of lavender. He was lying on a clean bed, and the child who was reading to him was following the words with his finger. He was no older than seven.

'That's . . . where . . . the k-k . . . um, the key . . . was hid-den,' he went on, not realising that Tomek had opened his eyes and was looking at him.

'The cocro . . . the cro-co-dile . . . was . . . sound . . . asleep. "Now is my . . . chance . . ." thought Flibus . . . the little . . . monkey.'

Tomek couldn't help smiling. The child was putting all his heart into his reading, but he stumbled over almost every word. The window was half open, and the lace curtains billowed in the breeze. It was evening, probably, or twilight at any rate. Outside, the bare branches of a tree were reaching up to the sky. *Hmm*, thought Tomek, *its leaves have already fallen . . .*

The furniture in the bedroom comprised of a simple little wardrobe, a sink, a bedside table and a chair on which the child was sitting, with a fat book on his knees.

'And he . . . advanced . . . imper-per . . . impre-step . . . Oh drat! Imperspres . . .'

'Imperceptibly . . . ?' murmured Tomek, coming to his aid.

It was as if a bomb had exploded in the room. The child's jaw opened wide, he dropped the huge book onto the floor and rushed out of the open door as fast as his legs would carry him.

'Wait!' shouted Tomek, but the boy had already disappeared.

He sat up in bed and leaned against the pillow. That simple movement made him feel giddy. *I've slept for too long*, he thought, *but where am I now?* Gradually his memory came back to him: he'd left the village . . . because of the bears . . . Yes, that was it . . . because of the blind bears . . . no, that wasn't it . . . because of the flowers . . . yes, because of the flowers . . . there was a donkey too . . . whose name was . . . whose name was . . .

The donkey's name was on the tip of his tongue when he heard voices coming from downstairs. Then at least ten people were jostling one another on the stairs: 'Let me through! Don't push! I want to see him! So do I!'

Finally, a loud voice rose above the others: 'Quiet! You'll frighten him. You'll go in when I say you can!'

Peace was restored. The stairs creaked a little, then a shape appeared in the doorway. Despite the darkness, Tomek saw that it was a very tiny old man with a white beard. He walked towards Tomek's bed with a kindly smile and opening his arms, said 'Welcome among us.'

'Who are you?' Tomek asked weakly. 'Where am I?'

'You are in the perfume-makers' village,' replied the old man. 'My name is Eztergom and I am the chief. We were hunting for new fragrances in the meadow, and we came across you fast asleep, so we brought you back here. But don't be afraid, you are safe. Look, your belongings have been put away in this wardrobe.'

He opened the wardrobe so that Tomek could see he was speaking the truth. 'I'm sure you have a thousand questions you want to ask me, and I'll happily answer them later. But first of all I'd like the villagers to be able to see you . . . awake. It's tradition, and it would make them very happy. Do you have any objections?'

'But . . . not at all . . . on the contrary,' stammered Tomek, who was utterly perplexed. 'It would make me happy too . . .'

'Thank you very much indeed,' said the old man, who scuttled over to the door and beckoned to those waiting on the stairs.

The room immediately filled with men, women and

children who all looked like Eztergom, short with big round heads and chubby cheeks. And they all had the same disarming smile as the old man. They approached timidly, without a sound, gazing at him as tenderly as if he were a newborn baby. Since Tomek didn't know how to react, he merely nodded his thanks. The group soon left, and another took its place, then another, and then another. Last of all came the child who had been reading to him earlier. Eztergom motioned to him to come right up to the bed, and introduced him: 'This is young Atchigom. It's thanks to him that you are awake.'

The young Atchigom in question was bursting with a mixture of pride and embarrassment. His cheeks were flushed and his eyes were shining with delight.

'Thank you, Atchigom,' said Tomek, without knowing exactly what he was thanking him for.

'And now,' concluded Eztergom, 'I'm going to wait for you in the dining hall. Our cooks are making a delicious meal for you. Do you like pancakes? Take your time to wake up properly and get dressed. Atchigom will stay downstairs by the door and show you the way when you're ready.'

Then the two of them turned on their heel and disappeared, leaving Tomek alone. He didn't know what to think. He did indeed have lots of questions to ask Eztergom! He got out of bed and tottered unsteadily over to the window. The village was built on a hill, and he could see the beginnings of the meadow below. But there were no flowers . . .

Tomek opened the wardrobe. All his clothes had been washed and ironed. Even his shoes had been polished. His blanket was there too, neatly folded, as well as his bear knife, his waterskin and his two embroidered handkerchiefs.

Waiting downstairs by the door, he found Atchigom, who proudly escorted him through the village.

'It was me who woke you! It's me who'll be beside you tomorrow in the carriage!'

'In the carriage? We'll be in a carriage?'

Tomek would have liked to know more, but they had already reached the dining hall and the child skipped off happily. Eztergom invited Tomek to sit down and immediately they were served a jug of cider and a pile of pancakes. There were savoury ones with bacon or cheese and sweet ones with honey, apple or jam.

'Eat your fill, my dear friend,' said the old man. 'And while you're eating, I'll tell you everything you want to know. Because you must be finding all this very mysterious.'

'Yes, I am,' replied Tomek, and was all ears.

'You inhaled the scent of the huge blue flowers called "sails" because of their size,' explained Eztergom. 'They look as if they're floating in water.'

'Yes,' recalled Tomek, 'I saw them . . .'

'Those flowers send anyone who breathes in their smell into a deep sleep. And they sleep until someone speaks aloud the Awakening Words. A little cider?'

'The Awakening Words? What Awakening Words?' asked Tomek, forgetting to eat and drink.

'Exactly! No one knows. The words are different for each person. Now, let's see: what were the words you heard as you woke up?'

'It was *crocodile*,' Tomek recalled.

'No,' said Eztergom. 'That would have been too easy, we would have found it much sooner. There were probably other words . . .'

'*Under the belly of the crocodile*, I think. Yes, that's it, Atchigom was saying: *Under the belly of the crocodile* when I woke up.'

'That's it,' exulted the old man: '*Under the belly of the crocodile* . . . So for you, and for no one else, the Awakening Words are *Under the belly of the crocodile*!'

'But that's impossible to think of!' exclaimed Tomek. 'How did Atchigom come across them?'

'By chance, my friend, pure chance! Please try these bacon pancakes, otherwise our cooks will be offended!'

Tomek helped himself and bit into the pancake. It was deliciously soft and tasty.

'You see,' Eztergom went on, 'we take turns to sit by the bedside of the slumberer and we read non-stop until the Awakening Words are uttered. That's all. We have a very big library. So we choose the books one at a time and read aloud. Every single one of us – men, women and children – volunteers. No question of wasting a single minute. This can take a long time, but we always find the right words . . .'

'A long time?' muttered Tomek, suddenly feeling giddy. 'So how long was I asleep for?'

'You slept for three months and ten days . . .'

'Three months and . . .' repeated Tomek in disbelief. 'And . . . I ate nothing during all that time?'

'No,' smiled Eztergom, 'but since you weren't using up any energy, you didn't need to . . . are you ravenous?'

'Yes, I am a little,' replied Tomek, helping himself to a maple syrup pancake.

'You *did* sleep for quite a while, it's true, but sometimes it's much quicker. The young lady, for instance . . .'

'The young lady!' Tomek said with a start.

'Yes. The day before Prestigom and Foulgom found you, we rescued this young girl from the meadow, asleep like you. Almost every year, when the weather's sunny, we bring back careless travellers. And then we have to—'

'But where is she now?' broke in Tomek, his heart racing. 'Is she still asleep?'

'Oh no! With her we were very lucky. We found the Awakening Words on the third day. They were quite simply: *Once upon a time*. To think! *Once upon a time!* Too easy! She was a delightful girl, that girl. And kind too. Half of the village boys fell in love with her, and when she left, several of them were heartbroken.'

'Really?' stuttered Tomek, turning red. 'And did . . . did she leave as soon as she woke up?'

'Not at all. She stayed for more than a week. She enjoyed being here.'

'But . . . what did she do?'

'What did she do? It's very simple: she read to you. She spent nearly all her time doing so.'

'Oh, really?' said Tomek, deeply moved.

He imagined the girl sitting beside him and reading. What a pity she hadn't found the Awakening Words! On opening his eyes, he'd have seen her sitting at his bedside instead of Atchigom! Then they could have continued their journey together! But he had carried on sleeping and she had lost heart. Where could she be now, after all this time?

'Did you know this person?' asked Eztergom.

'Yes . . . no . . . I mean she came into my shop once,' replied Tomek. 'I run a grocery in my village . . .'

They finished eating, then the old man showed Tomek the library.

'Here,' he said, pointing to his left where a hundred or so books were set aside, 'these are all the books we read to you. Hannah read at least a dozen of them on her own.'

'Hannah?' said Tomek, wistfully.

'Yes, Hannah. The girl was called Hannah. Didn't you know?'

'No. I didn't . . .'

'And these,' Eztergom went on, pointing to the other books to his right, 'these are the books we would have read if you hadn't woken up!'

Tomek scanned the shelves. There were more than ten thousand books!

'But have you ever had to do that?' he said, 'I mean, read all of them?'

'Yes, once,' replied Eztergom. 'But that was a very long time ago, when I was still a child. We read for six years, two months and four days to awaken a good man called Mortimer. The Awakening Words were *Slipper, slipper*! The same word, twice in a row! *You* try to find that in a book!'

'So how did you manage it?'

'Well, in despair, we sent Tzergom, who was a sweet boy but a slow learner who didn't know how to read yet. We took him into the room and asked him to say whatever came into his head. Within ten minutes Mortimer was awake!'

They both laughed heartily. Eztergom's eyes creased agreeably when he laughed. He reminded Tomek of Isham and he felt a pang.

Then Eztergom yawned. It was late now, and he probably wanted to go to bed. Tomek, on the other hand, wasn't at all sleepy. He asked if he could spend the rest of the night in the library. Eztergom gladly gave him permission and arranged to meet him the next day.

'I'll show you around our perfume factory in the morning,' he said on leaving, 'and the big Awakening Celebration will take place in the afternoon, as is the custom. I wish you a very good night.'

'Good night to you too, Mr Eztergom,' replied Tomek.

The old man turned around once again. 'Oh my goodness, I almost forgot. The little lady left a letter for you. Here it is. It looks very long. It will take you most of the night to read it . . .'

CHAPTER NINE

Hannah

Right in the very centre of the library stood a huge stove, which was still warm. Tomek added a few logs, then settled himself comfortably at a little table lit by an oil lamp. The envelope was indeed fat, and he opened it carefully, taking out a dozen sheets of paper folded in four. The paper gave off a faint scent of violets. *The villagers must have given it to her*, thought Tomek, and he began to read.

> *Dear Mr Grocer,*
>
> *Forgive me for calling you that, but I don't know your name. I only know that it begins with a T, because of your embroidered handkerchiefs. My name is Hannah. I didn't tell you that when I came to buy barley sugar. This morning I read to you from the big book of* The Thousand and One Nights, *a story about crocodiles. And you appeared to stir a little. I thought for a moment that I'd found the Awakening Words. I was*

*happy and I tried everything I could think of: the
crocodile's head, crocodile teeth, the crocodile's belly . . .
but it was no use. You were still asleep. I saw your
waterskin in the cupboard. Are you looking for the water
of the River Qjar, like me? It would be lovely to go there
together. I don't like travelling on my own because there
are a lot of dangers along the way, as I've realised. But I
must go on. I can't wait for you to wake up.*

*Mr Eztergom told me about a person who slept
for six years, so . . . I have to carry on because I
desperately need some of that water. Just a few drops
will be enough, because it's for a bird. A bird so tiny
that she fits into the palm of my hand. I will put just a
single drop in her beak and that will be enough, I
think. You must be very surprised, naturally, because
you don't know my story. So here it is. You are the first
person I am telling it to.*

*My father was already old when I came into the
world and he was mad with joy at my birth. He had
four more sons after me, but he barely noticed, I fear.
I was the apple of his eye, his princess, his life.
Nothing was too fine for me. He gave me the most
precious fabrics, the rarest jewels. My mother berated
him for it, but he wouldn't listen. We lived in a town in
the north, whose name won't mean anything to you.
Unless you are interested in birds, because it's where,
for one week every year, in the spring, the biggest of all*

73

bird markets is held. You find species from all over the world, and people come from far and wide. My father used to take me there every year, holding me in his arms for fear of losing me. And every year, he would ask me the same question: 'Which bird would you like, Hannah? Which one would please you?'

I'd choose the one I liked best, because of its colours, or its song, or both. And my father would buy it without ever looking at the price. I'd put it in my big cage with the others. The birds were my greatest joy. When I turned six, my father took me to the market as usual: 'Which bird would you like, Hannah? Which one would please you?'

I pointed to a brilliantly coloured little songbird. But the seller was asking a very high price. When my father expressed his surprise, he said that this songbird was actually a princess who had lived more than a thousand years ago and who had been bewitched and turned into a bird. That was why he wouldn't sell her for a penny less.

Anyone else would have realised that this man was a swindler. But my father simply told the seller to keep the bird for him and that he would be back soon. In less than a week, he had sold all his belongings: our animals, our house, our land, our furniture and even the bedsheets. Despite that, he was still short of around half of the sum needed. Then he borrowed the money from a moneylender. We went back to the seller *and bought the bird. My mother left us the very next day, taking my brothers with her. We never saw them again. They took everything that was left in the house with them, even the birds. They left only the little songbird. We moved into a shack. My father hired himself out as a human carthorse: he pulled carriages through the town's streets. The streets are on a steep slope and he soon grew weak because of his age. The money he earned was barely enough for us to live on. And yet he carried on taking me to the bird market every year and asking the usual question: 'Which bird would you like, Hannah? Which one would please you?' Since we were too poor even to buy a sparrow, I said I didn't want one, that I was happy with my songbird. My father died of exhaustion after three years, but I don't think he regretted what he'd done for a single moment. He was mad, of course, but it was a very gentle, quiet madness. He went mad with joy the day I was born and he remained mad, and that's the truth. Nothing else mattered for him. I was taken in by distant relatives who were very good to me and I lived with them until now. Of my past life, I have nothing left, except the little songbird. I look at her and I hear my father asking: 'Which bird would you like, Hannah? Which one would please you?'*

And then one morning, when I got up, I found her under her perch, shivering with fever. I warmed her, stroked her and scolded her too, because she couldn't leave me all alone. I had never believed, of course, what the seller had said, but since my songbird hadn't changed at all with time, I ended up believing that maybe she would live for a thousand years. But her colours were growing dull, she sang less often. She was becoming . . . old.

I don't want my bird to die. I don't!

One day a storyteller came to our town and I went to listen to him in the square. He spoke of the River Ojar which flows backwards and upside down and whose water stops people from ever dying. He explained that although this river was hard to reach it really did exist, somewhere in the south. People claimed it wasn't true because that gave them a good excuse not to look for it. They simply didn't have the courage, that's all. In other words, he said exactly what I needed to hear to convince me to set out to find it!

I left our house one night at the very beginning of summer. I woke my little sister, who's six (she's the daughter of my adoptive parents but I call her my little sister because I'm very fond of her). I told her I was going away for a while and asked her to take good care of my songbird and to give everyone a kiss for me, and that I'd be back soon. Then I took a few clothes, my savings, and I escaped through my bedroom window.

Before wandering into your grocery by chance, I had had lots of incredible adventures. I'll tell you about them one day, perhaps. Did you come through that terrible forest full of bears? At any rate, like me you must have crossed the meadow and breathed in the scent of those flowers called sails, because you're here, sleeping soundly as I write. What else awaits us before we reach the River Qjar? What dangers lie in store? All this so that one day, perhaps, I'll be able to put a drop of water in a bird's beak . . . Who can understand that? You?

Heaven knows where I'll be when you read this letter. I'm giving it to Mr Eztergom because I'm worried someone might take it if I leave it on your bedside table. I probably shouldn't have told you my secret, I barely know you. And yet I don't regret it. I trust you and I will leave with a lighter heart tomorrow morning. Maybe we'll meet again, and this time you'll be more talkative, I hope!

Hannah

PS: What's in that little pouch around your neck?

Tomek, half laughing and half crying, took the coin out of its pouch and clenched it in his hand.

'It's a farthing,' he replied. 'I'll give it back to you soon.'

CHAPTER TEN

Pepigom

It was barely daylight when Eztergom came to fetch Tomek.

'I thought I'd find you awake, which is why I have come so early.'

They started with a copious breakfast, then they walked over to the perfume factory, which was far bigger than Tomek would ever have imagined. It employed at least three hundred people, almost the entire population of the village, and was made up of several buildings. The first was the store for the dried flowers which the pickers had gathered the previous summer. They were still brightly coloured, and it was a wonder to walk among the multicoloured vats. In another building, the flowers were pressed, crushed and ground. Each person looked as if they were putting their heart into their work, and they sang to keep up their spirits even more. The third building was the distillery. The men and women working there wore white chemists' coats.

'And now,' announced Eztergom with pride, 'I invite you to step inside a place where few people are permitted to enter. It is our secret laboratory. Here, we make absolutely unique fragrances. Do come in.'

They were greeted by a plump, smiling girl whose nose and face were studded with freckles. Eztergom introduced her, saying, 'Master Tomek, this is Miss Pepigom. Despite her young age, she is one of the most important people in this perfume factory, because she has the best nose of all of us. It is a talent that deteriorates with age and it is rare for anyone to be able to do this job once they are over forty. But Pepigom is particularly young and brilliant. How old are you, Miss?'

'I'm fourteen and three months,' replied the girl confidently.

Tomek thought that fourteen wasn't *that* young, but since Eztergom said so . . .

'Miss Pepigom,' continued the old man, 'would it be possible for you to reveal some of the team's latest discoveries to our friend?'

'With pleasure, Mr Eztergom. I am honoured.'

'Then I'll leave him with you. I must go, because I have to write my speech for this afternoon's big event.'

Pepigom showed Tomek into an adjoining room where hundreds of small bottles stood in rows on shelves. She picked one up and removed the stopper. 'Breathe in, Master Tomek, and tell me what it smells of.'

Tomek recognised a pleasant lemon scent, and told her so.

'That's right. What about this one?'

Tomek had to guess three times before he could identify the smell of woodland moss.

'Excellent, Master Tomek. You have an exceptional nose. But let me tell you that thanks to our research and trials with different blends, we manage to create very special, very subtle perfumes. Let's see if you can recognise them.'

In spite of her fourteen years, Pepigom barely came up to Tomek's shoulder. She smelled deliciously of fresh verbena and, like everyone in the village, she was plump and radiated kindness. Tomek inhaled deeply from the bottle she was holding out to him, but this time he was stumped, completely stumped. He even had the impression that this bottle smelled of nothing at all. Instead of concentrating, he allowed himself to be distracted and started daydreaming. He saw himself sitting by a pond. It was long ago, when his parents were alive. They had picnicked there, but the rain had driven them away. Why was he remembering that now?'

'Well?' asked Pepigom, smiling.

'I don't know,' confessed Tomek, trying to wrench himself away from his daydream. 'I can't smell . . . anything at all.'

'Really? And your mind was perhaps elsewhere instead of thinking about it?'

'Yes, that's exactly right!' said Tomek, surprised. 'Please forgive me.'

'And can you tell me exactly what you were thinking about? Was it a pond, and raindrops?'

Tomek, gobsmacked, was at a loss for words. Could this girl read his mind?

On seeing his astonishment, Pepigom burst out laughing.

'This perfume is called First Raindrops on the Pond.'

'Oh,' was all Tomek could say. 'That . . . that's . . . amazing. Truly.'

'Now try this one and tell me what it is,' suggested Pepigom, holding out another bottle.

It only took Tomek a few seconds to visualise an image, but it sounded so silly he was reluctant to say anything. 'A . . . a hill . . . musicians . . . crowds of people . . . songs . . .'

'Well done!' exclaimed Pepigom. 'But there's something else too. Have another try.'

Tomek sniffed several times and the music played faster and faster, everyone was dancing and cheering. Yes, it was a wedding! Then he realised that the bride and groom, enthroned on a seat surrounded by their friends, were no other than *them*, Tomek and Pepigom, arms entwined and kissing under a shower of flower petals!

'A . . . wedding?' stammered Tomek, blushing.

'Well done again! You'll definitely be taking over my job soon! This perfume is called Wedding on the Hill. Do you want to continue?'

'Happily,' replied Tomek, who was beginning to find this game intriguing.

And so, one by one, he inhaled the following perfumes: Birth of a Lamb in Fresh Straw, Setting off on a Journey at Dawn, Reading a Letter Written by a Loved one, Making a Pyramid out of Craft Sticks at the Kitchen Table when it's Snowing Outside . . . and lots more besides.

'But tell me,' he asked after a while, 'do you only make pleasing fragrances?'

'Oh yes, of course,' replied Pepigom. 'Life's too short to waste it on nasty things, Master Tomek.'

'Certainly,' agreed Tomek, and he entirely shared her view.

At lunchtime, he ate with Eztergom.

This time there were doughnuts that were just as delicious as the pancakes. No wonder the perfume makers were so well-fed, thought Tomek, they only eat good things.

Once they'd had their dessert – yummy blueberry

tart – they left the dining hall. Tomek thought he must be dreaming: at the very moment he appeared at the top of the staircase, a single roar erupted from the mouths of the hundreds of villagers gathered in the square. 'Hurrah!'

And straight away, wildly joyful music started playing. The little trumpet players blew as if their cheeks would burst, while the drummers were going wild. A real carriage stood waiting at the bottom of the staircase, drawn by four white ceremonial ponies with plumes and tassels. The carriage roof was in the shape of a giant crocodile, and *under the belly of the crocodile* sat the young Atchigom, all dressed up. He cut a fine figure in his golden tunic and top hat. Tomek took his place beside him and the carriage set off. They rode through the village streets to cheering and cries of 'Bravo!'.

I don't deserve all this, thought Tomek. But after all, the people looked so happy to honour him that it would have been churlish to refuse. Atchigom, sitting beside him, was lapping it all up. Laughing, he plunged his hands into a bucket of confetti which he scattered over the spectators. They soon arrived at the town hall, where Eztergom awaited them at the top of the steps.

When the carriage had stopped, the old man raised his arms to silence the crowd and gave the following speech: 'Dear friends, we are gathered here once again for the great Awakening Celebration. I should be used to it by now, because this is not my first, but each time, I am overcome with emotion. Master Tomek came back to life, he was reborn among us. May he be our child, like all those who have gone before him. I shall not say any more, because I dislike long speeches, and so do you. Long live Master Tomek! Long live Atchigom, who awakened him! And long live you all, my friends!'

With that, he took a big handkerchief out of his pocket and blew his nose noisily. Many of the spectators did the same. The women were nearly all crying. The men sniffled. Only the children yelled exuberantly: 'Long live!' Because for them, this was all simply a game.

To bring the ceremony to a close, Eztergom gave Tomek a medal on which was engraved:

TO MASTER TOMEK,
FROM THE PERFUME MAKERS

He was expected to say a few words too, of course, but he was so emotional that all he could stammer was: 'Th-thank you everyone ... I-I thank you from the bottom of my heart.'

And the crowd burst into applause to save him from embarrassment.

The afternoon was a joyous affair. On every street corner, people were playing games of skill or performing trials of strength: here they were lifting tree stumps, over there they were throwing rag balls at puppets to knock them over. There was a sack race, and an egg-and-spoon race (competitors ran with a wooden spoon in their mouths balancing an egg). And everywhere was laughter and good humour.

That night, there was a lavish banquet in the dining hall, followed by a ball, and cider ran freely. Tomek had to dance with all the village girls until his legs couldn't hold him up any more. As soon as he said goodbye to one at the end of a dance, another leaped into his arms. And Pepigom was far from being the last . . .

Around midnight, he was finally able to go back to his room, and he dropped down onto the bed fully clothed, feeling slightly giddy. *My goodness*, he thought, before falling asleep, *what a strange journey this is! How on earth will I tell people about it when I go back home?*

CHAPTER ELEVEN

Snow

When Tomek opened his eyes the next day, it was already late morning and snowflakes were whirling outside his window. He leaped out of bed and saw that a thick blanket of snow had fallen over the village during the night.

Just my luck, he thought. *Now how will I be able to leave?*

The previous day, he had planned to say goodbye to his new friends as early as possible because he had already lost enough time. While he had been peacefully sleeping, Hannah had continued on her journey. Where was she now?

He put on a coat that had been left over the back of the chair for him and, outside his door, he even found a pair of fur-lined boots that were just his size. He plodded through deep snow to the dining hall, in the hope of finding someone there, but it was empty at that hour. Everyone must already be at work. So he went to the library and was glad to come across old Eztergom, absorbed in a book.

'Hello, Mr Eztergom,' he said. 'I was hoping to leave today, but with all this snow . . .'

Eztergom flashed him a broad smile and invited him to sit down beside him: 'I fear you may have to stay with us for some time, my young friend. Winter here is long and harsh. This snow won't melt, and there is still a lot more to come. Our village is going to be cut off. No one will be able to enter it or leave until the fine weather returns. But don't worry, we know how to entertain ourselves and keep our spirits up. The time will pass very quickly, you'll see.'

'But how long does your winter last?' asked Tomek, his voice quavering. 'When will I be able to leave?'

'Spring will come in around four months, and it's a glorious season here, just you wait.'

Tomek had to make a huge effort not to burst into tears. Four months! Four months moping around here! Never would he be able to wait such a long time. He would die of boredom and impatience first! Since he couldn't hide his despair, he decided to confide the real reasons to Eztergom. Otherwise, the old man might have thought that he wasn't happy in the village. And that was too unfair. So he told him the whole story. Eztergom listened closely, then placed his hand on Tomek's shoulder. 'Now I understand your impatience, my young friend. But don't be downhearted. You might even be sad to leave when the time comes.'

'I'm sure I will,' replied Tomek, trying to smile. 'I'm sure I will.' But his eyes were full of tears.

'As for this River Qjar,' the old man went on, 'I can tell you that it does indeed exist, if that makes you feel a little better. And it does indeed begin in the ocean, only . . .'

'Only?' asked Tomek.

'Only . . . not on this shore . . .'

'What? You mean first I have to cross the ocean?'

'Unfortunately, yes,' confirmed Eztergom. 'But I'll tell you more about it another time . . .'

During the following days, despite everyone's attempts to cheer him up and despite his own efforts to appear content, Tomek felt down in the dumps. He spent most of his time in the library or in his room, mulling over gloomy thoughts. Then, as Eztergom had predicted, there were more heavy snowfalls and soon it was only possible to move around through a maze of trenches shovelled out between the houses. The village had become a giant white labyrinth, where the children played at slithering on their backs and popping up in front of you on street corners. Then Tomek finally accepted the idea that this was simply how it was, and he would have to wait. And so there was no point in being miserable. Sadness was rude, he told himself, and he resolved to think more of others and a little less of himself.

Most of the villagers ate in the dining hall because they didn't like staying at home on their own. Often in the evenings, after supper, they played cards or ludo, made music or improvised plays. Tomek quickly realised that the perfume makers loved clowning around, adored acting, singing and most of all, drinking cider. He gradually recovered his good humour.

During the daytime, he wandered around the perfume factory and visited Pepigom, who jumped for joy each time: 'Oh, Master Tomek! How kind of you to come and see us!'

She would often invite him to sniff a new fragrance or ask his opinion.

'Do you think it smells more like When Several People Are Looking at an Anthill, or When One Person Looks at an Anthill on Their Own?'

Tomek would give his view. They had a lot of fun, because it took very little for Pepigom to burst out laughing.

Three months had gone by when, one afternoon, Tomek was told he should go to the library, where Eztergom was waiting for him. And there the old man was, in the company of a ginger-bearded fellow almost

Tomek's height, which was very tall for someone from the village.

'Tomek, my boy, let me introduce Bastibalagom. He's our sea captain. I thought for a long time before inviting you to this little meeting, but I think it is necessary. You are a determined lad, as your long and perilous journey here proves. There would probably be no point trying to dissuade you from continuing, would there?'

'No, there wouldn't,' said Tomek. 'I have every intention of carrying on.'

'As I thought. That's why, since we can't keep you here, I have decided to help you. If you wish, you will set sail in the spring with our crew. But before you do, I would like you to be aware of the risks involved. And so I asked our good captain to come here. He will explain better than I can. Over to you, Bastibalagom.'

The man with the ginger beard cleared his throat several times, then spoke: 'My young friend, you probably know already that our perfumes are absolutely unique. They are our only source of wealth, so it is vital for us to sell them. The problem is, our best customers are on the other side of the ocean. So, every year, in the spring, we embark on the crossing. It requires a great deal of courage because we are never sure if we will succeed. Take a look at this logbook . . .'

And he opened a big book bound in ancient leather

and nudged it towards Tomek. There was a detailed drawing of a splendid three-master on the right-hand page, and you could even see the sailors on the deck.

'Look. On the left-hand page you'll see the year and the name of the ship. This one, the *Hope*, completed the voyage three times, before going down with all hands on board.'

Bastibalagom turned the page.

'This one, the *Darling*, only made it twice. This is the *Vigilant*, which made the return journey eight times under the orders of Captain Tolgom, an unequalled feat. And that is the *Pearl*, which never returned from its maiden voyage . . .'

Eztergom blew his nose noisily and Bastibalagom was silent for a few moments. The list of years and ships continued on the following pages, filling the entire book.

'And who are these people?' asked Tomek, pointing to the names written on the left-hand pages.

'They're the names of the captains and the sailors. We will never forget them.'

There was another silence.

Then Tomek asked the question that had been nagging at him for a while: 'And these *R*s, what do they mean? There are a lot of them . . .'

The two men exchanged glances. They were clearly uncomfortable.

'Well,' began Bastibalagom, 'that *R* means *rainbow*.'

'Rainbow?' parroted Tomek.

'Yes, it means that those ships vanished after sailing beneath a glorious rainbow. We don't know what became of them afterwards.'

'But how do you know about the rainbow, if no one has ever come back?' asked Tomek.

'Well, some have. A few sailors, terrified by the sight of the rainbow, took to the water in lifeboats and cast themselves adrift. Most perished, devoured by sharks most likely, but some did manage to reach dry land. Or they were rescued by passing ships. And those who returned all told exactly the same story: they saw their ship sailing directly towards the rainbow, without being able to change course, then fade from view and vanish for ever . . . There, now you know as much as we do and, when the time comes, you can make an informed decision whether to stay or leave.'

'All right,' said Tomek. 'I'm going to . . . think about it.'

'By the way,' added Bastibalagom, getting to his feet, 'I didn't tell you about the storms, the sharks and the pirates we sometimes have to fight off, but those are much less fearsome . . .'

With that, he shook Tomek's hand, then Eztergom's, and left.

*

The month leading up to the ship's departure sped by. Tomek knew that he would be leaving, and he had his heart set on spending as much time as he could with the villagers. One evening, in the dining hall, he confided in Pepigom and she looked extremely upset.

'I wish you could stay here,' she said, sadly pricking her bacon pancake with the prongs of her fork. 'We could become . . . good friends.'

They had already been good friends for a long time, thought Tomek. She meant something different, that was clear.

'I wish I could too . . .' he replied, turning red. 'But I'm . . . I'm already engaged.'

'Oh, really? To another girl from the village?'

'Oh no, not at all. To a girl from back home.'

'So maybe it's that Hannah who stayed here?'

Pepigom not only had a good nose, she also had a strong intuition.

'Yes, that's right, it's her,' replied Tomek, flustered.

'Well, congratulations. She's very pretty,' said Pepigom, with a half-hearted smile.

If Tomek had dared, he would have given her a hug to comfort her, but unfortunately there were still a lot of people at the tables around them and he couldn't.

'But I'm very fond of you too, Pepigom. You're the kindest girl I've ever met . . .'

He realised he was no longer calling her Miss

Pepigom. That made them laugh. Just then, the musicians launched into a lively tune and they both rose to dance.

A few days later came a mild spell. The snow thawed as quickly as it had arrived, and soon the meadow was covered in flowerbuds. The crew started going back and forth to ready the *Valiant* for the voyage. That was the name of the ship awaiting them at the end of a little creek. They loaded mainly food and clothes, and also board games, because the crossing could take more than a month. The crates of perfume were carefully stowed in the hold. On the day they set sail, the entire population walked down to the ocean to give the crew a send-off. Bastibalagom and his fourteen sailors went aboard, after hugging their loved ones. When they were all on deck, Eztergom, sitting astride a rock, took a sheet of paper out of his pocket on which he appeared to have written a long speech. He adjusted his spectacles and tried to read, but he was overcome with emotion and couldn't speak. In the end, he simply shouted, 'I wish you a safe voyage, my friends!' and folded up his sheet of paper again.

Everyone shouted: 'Safe voyage!' and waved white handkerchiefs.

Pepigom gave Tomek a little bottle of perfume.

'I blended it for you. But please don't open it before you leave.'

This time, ignoring the crowd around them, Tomek hugged her and pressed her plump little body to him.

'Thank you, Pepigom. Don't worry, I'll be back.'

And he ran onto the ship. It was high tide now, and the sailors hoisted the white sails. The *Valiant* immediately caught the wind and sped straight towards the high seas, while in the west, the sun sank below the horizon, casting its last flaming rays over the waters.

CHAPTER TWELVE

Bastibal

Tomek had a tiny cabin all to himself. As soon as he had settled in, he took from his pocket the little bottle Pepigom had given him, removed the stopper and sniffed. The scent it released was not Hannah's, because she didn't wear any. But the amazing thing was, breathing it in was enough to conjure up her entire person. How had Pepigom achieved such a miracle? Tomek raised the bottle to his nostrils again and once more he saw the musicians and dancers at the celebration on the hill, but this time, sitting beside him, surrounded by their friends and beneath the shower of flower petals, was no longer Pepigom but a radiant Hannah herself, and she was kissing him . . .

Thank you, Pepigom! Tomek said inwardly. *You are a good person.*

In the days that followed, the weather stayed fine and the ocean calm. The wind filled the sails and the *Valiant* raced along. Since navigating in these waters was easy, the sailors took the opportunity to teach Tomek a few techniques. He particularly enjoyed climbing up the foremast and gazing out over the vast blue expanse. Everything was so peaceful and reassuring that it was hard to imagine there could be the slightest danger. He was even allowed to take the helm, under Bastibalagom's supervision, and each time was a chance to chat to him.

'How did you become a captain, Mr Bastibalagom?' Tomek asked one day.

'Oh, it's a long story! I'm not from the perfume-makers' village. I'm like you, I come from elsewhere.'

Tomek was flabbergasted.

'Oh, really? I didn't know . . .'

'I come from across the ocean. My real name is Bastibal. But when I decided to spend the rest of my life in the perfume-makers' village, over thirty years ago now, I changed my name to Bastibalagom. I thought it had a nice ring to it – what do you think?'

'Oh yes, definitely! Bastibalagom is a fine name.'

'Isn't it? As for Bastibal, he no longer exists. It's better that way . . .'

Tomek wanted to ask *why* it was better that way, but was afraid of prying.

The old captain probably guessed it.

'Perhaps you'd like to hear my story? I'll gladly tell

you if you're interested. We have all the time in the world and the sea is calm.'

Tomek accepted enthusiastically and Bastibalagom began: 'You see, Tomek, you seem like a nice boy to me, whereas when I was your age, I was a scallywag. A bad egg, as they say. Not a day went by without someone saying, "Bastibal, if you're lucky, you'll end up in prison, if you're not so lucky, you'll swing!" Why was I like that? I don't know. It was "in the blood", as they used to say. One day, my father took me to a draper's shop. "Bastibal," he said, "this man is my best friend and he's offered to take you on as an apprentice. He knows you've been in trouble, but he's prepared to turn a blind eye. This is a great opportunity for you, you realise?" and, as we reached the door to the shop, he took my hands in his, looked me straight in the eyes and said: "I know what people say about you, but it makes no difference to me. You are my son, Bastibal, and you always will be, and I have faith in you."

'A few days later, the draper repeated almost the same thing with almost the same words: "I don't care what people say about you, Bastibal, you're a good lad and I have faith in you." Perhaps I just needed someone to talk to me like that. The fact remains that I changed overnight. You couldn't have found a more hardworking and conscientious apprentice than me. After barely two weeks, the draper entrusted me with the key to the till. And what do you think I did, Tomek?'

Since Tomek didn't know what to reply, Bastibalagom shook his head at length, then said, 'Well, I ran off with it.'

'With . . . the key?' Tomek asked innocently.

Bastibalagom burst out laughing.

'No, with the till! With the till . . . What do you expect, it's like saying to a hen, "I trust you, hen, stop laying eggs!" The hen says "All right," she controls herself for a day or two and then, when she's had enough, what does the hen do, Tomek?'

'She lays an egg?'

'That's right, she lays an egg. And me, I ran off with the till. I walked across the fields for days and days. At night, I slept in barns or cowsheds with the animals. But the worst thing was my shame, of course. The till was heavy, and, in the end, I threw it into a ravine. Then I walked to the ocean. I came across two fishing boats. I stole one and put out to sea . . . you asked me how I became a captain, Tomek. Well, I became one at that moment, probably. But a strange captain who, once on the high seas, began to cry and call out for his mother. I was the loneliest person in the world, in the middle of the ocean, in that boat that I was no longer even steering. I had nothing to eat or drink. Night fell and I was freezing. I said to myself, "I'm going to jump into the water and put an end to it all!" And do you know why I didn't?'

'Because you still hoped to be rescued?' ventured Tomek.

'Not at all. I didn't jump overboard to kill myself because I didn't know how to swim! That's ridiculous, isn't it?'

And Bastibalagom hooted with laughter again.

'And how did it end?' asked Tomek.

'Well, at dawn, I woke up in the arms of some little men who were hauling me up onto their sailing boat. They wrapped me in blankets, made me drink hot milk and gave me bacon pancakes. You will have gathered that they were the little perfume makers who were returning home. Their ship was called the *Vigilant*, and their captain was a certain Tolgom. I recall that the holds were crammed full of fabrics and cereals that they had been given in exchange for crates of perfume. They were happy and good-humoured, as they always are, as a matter of fact. They didn't ask me any questions. They simply took care of me as best they could. And that, Tomek, is how I arrived in their village and how I owe them my life. Since that day, I've been trying to show my gratitude . . .'

'And that's why you became a captain? Because it's dangerous?'

'You have understood perfectly. It's so dangerous that even the young sailors who make the voyage must be unmarried and childless.'

'Really?' murmured Tomek, alarmed. 'And . . . there are still volunteers?'

'Volunteers? By the shovel load!' exclaimed Bastibalagom. 'The perfume makers look like children with their round faces and their short stature, but they are incredibly brave, and they are all prepared to sacrifice themselves for their community.'

But there was still one question that was worrying Tomek.

'Because you've crossed the ocean so many times, Mr Bastibalagom, have you ever been back home? Did you ever see your parents again?'

'I don't know if I should reply yes or no,' said the captain with a wistful smile. 'Three years ago, we went to sell our perfumes in the little town I come from. It is at the foot of a hill. I stayed up on the hill for several days before I found the courage to go down to the town. Just think, I hadn't been back for nearly thirty years! One evening, an old man was walking along the path. I had a premonition, and I hid up a tree. It was my father. Even though he was very old by then, I still recognised him. He paused for a moment beneath the tree to gaze at our town. He looked sad and pensive. I was sitting on a branch, just six feet above his head. He couldn't see me.

For a second, I thought of jumping down and saying, "Hello, Papa, it's me . . ." But I was forty, and at forty, you don't jump down from a tree saying, "Hello, Papa, it's me . . ." So I simply silently asked him to forgive me for all the grief I'd probably caused him and my mother. After a few minutes, he continued slowly on his way. In my tree, I watched him shuffle off and I was Bastibal once more, the young boy from long ago. I even shed a little tear, I can tell you – I'm not ashamed of it. Then some of my men came by and I jumped down from my branch. I was Captain Bastibalagom again, I had to be. That's life, Tomek, my friend . . .'

On that note, a slightly more powerful wave crashed against the ship, soaking both of them, which put an end to their conversation.

It was the next day, at around nine o'clock in the morning, that a cabin boy came and gave three little knocks on Tomek's door.

'All hands on deck, captain's orders!'

Tomek put on his shoes and went up immediately. The entire crew was already assembled. Tomek was the last to have been alerted, probably because he was only a passenger. The sailors were standing as still as statues. No one spoke. Straight ahead of the ship, a splendid rainbow formed a perfect, colourful arch in the azure sky.

Tomek moved like a sleepwalker, incapable of uttering a word.

At the helm, Bastibalagom turned to his men and spoke. 'Gentlemen, the tiller is no longer responding. Any manoeuvres are pointless, and we are heading directly towards the rainbow. The *Valiant* fought hard, but she is now being drawn in by an irresistible power. I don't know what is on the other side. All I know is that no one has ever returned. I release every one of you from your duties as of now. You may use the lifeboats to escape. But I must warn you that this part of the ocean is infested with sharks. You may also choose to remain on board. Whatever you do, I insist on praising your great courage, in my own name and on behalf of the perfume-makers' village. As for myself, I shall of course remain on board the *Valiant*. I advise those who wish to take to the water to do so quicky – I have the impression that we are gaining speed. Thank you for your attention, gentlemen.'

At first, the sailors didn't budge an inch. Then slowly, they drew closer together and put their arms round one another's shoulders, still looking straight ahead. Seeing that Tomek wasn't sure what to do, one of them invited him over. Bastibalagom came and joined their group himself, and it was thus, pressed close together, that they began to pass beneath the glittering vault of the rainbow.

CHAPTER THIRTEEN

The Island-That-Isn't

You couldn't imagine a more magical sight. The colours of the rainbow mingling with the sea-spray formed a mist of multicoloured droplets that cooled your face then burst into crystalline musical notes like the sound of a harp playing.

If this is the end, thought Tomek on hearing this celestial music, *then we certainly had a beautiful death . . .*

He noticed that several of the sailors had forgotten their fear and were smiling. Even though there wasn't a breath of wind, the *Valiant* ploughed through the waters and soon they had to turn around to see the rainbow. It was beginning to fade, to disintegrate. Eventually, it disappeared entirely. And when they looked in front of them again, they saw nothing but the ocean, calm and peaceful.

The *Valiant* glided on for a few minutes in the silence, then a sailor pointed ahead and said weakly, 'Land ahoy!'

The island didn't look hostile, quite the opposite. It was lush and green, and as they drew near, they could even see pretty huts that looked like Wendy houses. The *Valiant* headed unaided towards a little port where sailing boats were moored.

They were a few hundred yards away when Bastibalagom grabbed Tomek's arm and squeezed it, almost crushing it, and began to stammer, 'Good Lord . . . I don't believe it . . . I'm dreaming . . .'

Tomek wondered for a moment what could have given the captain such as shock, but he soon had the answer: the first boat was called the *Hope*, you could see the name on the hull, and the second was called the *Darling*. There they were, side by side, seemingly in perfect condition: the *Vigilant*, which had rescued young Bastibal long ago, the *Pearl*, which had never returned from its maiden voyage, the *Spark,* the *Frigate* and the *Oceanus* and so, so many others that had been thought to be lost for ever. The sailors were so dumbfounded that they didn't know how to react. They gawped, wide-eyed, wondering what would happen next. As they entered the port, around fifteen young women scurried away from the quayside and vanished. The only person left was a little girl, watching them. Tomek thought she looked very much like a little girl from the perfume-makers' village . . .

While the *Valiant* dutifully moored up alongside the

other sailing boats, Bastibalagom called to the girl from the deck, 'Tell me, child, what is this place?'

Instead of answering, she wheeled around and ran away.

Bastibalagom turned to face his men.

'I think she's gone to inform the inhabitants. We're going to stay on board and wait. We know nothing about this island, which isn't marked on any maps, so it is better to be cautious.'

They didn't have to wait long. After barely two minutes, a crowd of people came rushing down the slopes to the port. They wore sarongs or light dresses typical of hot countries. They were all jogging and waving their arms in greeting. When they were on the quayside, Tomek had the strange feeling that these people were both familiar to him and strangers. Many of the men resembled the little perfume makers so closely, it was hard to tell them apart, but others, as well as all the women and girls, were a good height and had finer features. All of a sudden, one of the sailors let out a cry: 'Bjorgom! My brother!'

With that, he jumped into the water and swam to the shore, where he fell into the arms of a young man who looked almost like his twin.

There was a second shout: 'Uncle! Uncle! It's me!'

And a second sailor dived into the clear water of the harbour. Then Bastibalagom ordered the gangplank to be lowered and they all began to disembark. Tomek stayed on deck and from there he was able to witness deeply moving scenes. One after the other, all the crew members were reunited with an uncle, a friend or a big brother – all loved ones they had believed lost for ever and mourned for a long time. And now they had unexpectedly found them on this unknown island and were able to embrace them . . . and each time there were tears and endless hugs. The most emotional reunion was perhaps that of Bastibalagom and Tolgom, the old captain of the *Vigilant*. They embraced for a long time.

When the initial emotion had subsided, they all went together up to the village which was on the other side of the hill, and the sailors were served a succulent meal in the shade of a palm tree. After the long weeks at sea, it was a joy to eat fresh vegetables, sink their teeth into juicy fruits and drink delicious palm wine. After dessert, they split up, with each newcomer going to a host family's house. Tomek was the only person who didn't know anyone, so he followed his captain to Tolgom's. They sat on a mat, as the locals did, and a young woman brought them coffee.

'Dearest Bastibal,' began Tolgom, 'I owe you and our young friend Tomek some explanations. Let me tell you first of all that you are on the Island-That-Isn't.'

'The Island-That-Isn't? Curious name!' muttered

Bastibalagom. 'But it well and truly exists, because we're here!'

'Yes, it does exist for those of us who are here, but no one else knows about it. And if you like, I'll tell you why.'

Bastibalagom and Tomek were all ears.

'It seems this island has been inhabited since the dawn of time because it is particularly fertile and pleasant, as you will see. But it so happens that it is located at the exact centre of the ocean. Nowhere on Earth is there any land farther away from the rest of humanity. If it were to be marked on a map, it would be like a pinprick in the infinite ocean. The winds and currents are so strong that the rare ships that sail this way have always navigated around it without noticing it. There is nowhere more isolated than our Island-That-Isn't.'

'But all the same, we landed here . . .' ventured Tomek. 'How come?'

'You landed here because you were drawn here.'

'Oh . . . and who drew us here?'

'Our girls . . .' was all Tolgom replied, with an apologetic smile.

'Your girls?' chorused Bastibalagom and Tomek, baffled.

'Yes, our girls . . .' Tolgom went on. 'You see, a hundred years ago, a strange phenomenon occurred on the island: overnight, all the newborn babies were girls.

Not a single little boy. Don't ask me how or why, I don't know. That is how it was. At first, people thought that girls were worth just as much as boys, and they were often worth more, so why complain? But after a while, people began to worry. How could the population reproduce without men? Before each birth, everyone waited feverishly for the good news, until the midwife put her head around the door and uttered the fateful words: "It's a girl . . ." They scanned the horizon in the hope that a ship would come, but to no avail. More than twenty years went by.

'One day, a girl called Alma asked her mother what things had been like in the old days, when she was young, when there were boys. So her mother told her . . . She explained to her daughter how boys and girls were attracted to one another, how they courted. "You know," she said, "the boys always believed that they chose us, but actually, *we* were the ones who chose the boy who would choose us . . . That is how it has always been." And because Alma wanted to know more, her mother explained that a girl can bewitch a boy, simply because she wishes very hard to do so. Isn't that so, dear Bastibal, as you've probably experienced yourself?'

'N-no,' murmured Bastibalagom. 'I . . . I've stayed single . . .'

And Tomek was surprised to see him turn pink.

'In short,' went on Tolgom, 'from that day, Alma

had a bee in her bonnet, and she managed to rope in fourteen of her friends. One evening, they perched on a rock looking out over the ocean and they all looked in the same direction, hoping with every fibre of their being that a ship would come. And what do you think happened?'

'A ship came,' replied Tomek.

'Exactly! A ship came! Which hadn't happened for centuries! And there were fifteen sailors on board. You see how fate contrives things for the best. They married the fifteen young women, had children, only girls of course, and when *those* girls reached marriageable age in turn, they did as their mothers had done, and this practice still continues today. It's perfectly simple, isn't it?'

'But then,' said Tomek, dazed, 'is that how our boat was drawn here?'

Tolgom nodded.

'Absolutely. Maybe you saw the girls on the quayside when you arrived?'

'Yes, we did,' replied Tomek, recalling the fleeting forms glimpsed on the dock. 'But they ran away . . .'

'I'm not surprised!' said Tolgom. 'They're capable of attracting you from fifteen miles away and, once you're here, they are overcome with shyness and they scarper. It's the same every time!'

'If I understand you correctly,' Bastibalagom broke in timidly, 'these girls drew in our boat weighing several tonnes, "attracted" it, as you say, purely through the power of their thoughts. I have to say I find that hard to believe!'

'My dear Bastibal,' sighed Tolgom, 'you greatly underestimate the young ladies of this island. I know them well, and I am surprised by only one thing: how it is that the boats enter the harbour so smoothly and don't crash into its walls . . .'

'Oh,' was all the captain said, awestruck.

'Tell me, Mr Tolgom,' asked Tomek, 'how come all the sailors stayed here? Didn't any of them ever want to leave?'

At first, Tolgom hung his head and was silent. Then he looked from one to the other for a long time and finally said, with infinite sadness, 'My friends, welcome to our Island-That-Isn't. No one ever leaves here . . . Ever.'

CHAPTER FOURTEEN

A Riddle

'Well, I'm blowed!' exclaimed Bastibalagom after a moment, 'I'd like to see that with my own eyes! What could stop us from leaving if we wanted to?'

'Yes,' Tomek backed him up, 'we got ourselves here, so we'll find a way to leave . . .'

He tried to stay calm, but he was filled with a terrible anxiety.

'I understand your disbelief, my friends,' Tolgom went on, 'and first of all I must tell you that hundreds of sailors felt the same dismay on hearing those unbelievable words. But look at them after a few years: they're the happiest of men, they have wives and children and . . .'

'But that's not what it's about!' raged Bastibalagom. 'Tell us why it is supposedly impossible to leave this island! Has anyone even tried?'

'Alas, those who have tried are no longer of this world,' sighed Tolgom, 'but allow me instead to explain . . . Naturally you admired the rainbow that greets new arrivals to our Island-That-Isn't. It is one of the most beautiful sights that humans can set eyes upon, is it not? Well, that same rainbow forms as soon as a ship, a sailing boat, a rowing boat or even a raft moves away from the island and reaches the open sea. But when the vessel reaches it and is about to sail underneath, that magnificent rainbow turns black. There is no more terrifying sight than a black rainbow, I assure you. Then a thick mist rises, and nothing more happens. At least nothing that we can see from our island. One thing is certain: the vessel, big or small, ends up foundering and sinking to the bottom of the ocean. And it's been like this ever since all the babies were born as girls. It is a great mystery. Believe me, you'd do better to resign yourselves to learning to live here. You'll see: there's no milder climate than ours, we lack for nothing, we breed sheep and cows, the earth is fertile, and we grow every kind of . . .'

Tolgom carried on talking about his island, but Tomek and Bastibalagom had long since stopped listening.

In the late afternoon, they went for a walk. Tolgom took his two guests up to the top of the hill, and from there they could see that the Island-That-Isn't was indeed very small. It was dizzying to see how tiny it was surrounded by such immenseness. Tomek struggled to look pleased, but the idea of having to stay on this little patch of land for ever made him feel almost sick. And the beauty of the landscape made no difference.

His thoughts constantly returned to Hannah. How could he enjoy a future without the hope of seeing her again?

And Isham, to whom he'd promised he would return one day? And the water of the River Qjar that he meant to bring back for him?

That night, he found it impossible to get to sleep. He could hear Bastibalagom tossing and turning in the bedroom next door. He couldn't sleep either, and nor could the other sailors. In the space of a few hours, they had experienced so many powerful emotions! First of all terror at the sight of the deadly rainbow, then awe at its beauty, then the joy of being rescued, and the even greater joy at finding their loved ones alive, having given them up for dead long ago. And lastly, the terrible and unbelievable news that they were to stay for ever on this Island-That-Isn't. They couldn't decide whether that was wonderful, horrifying or both.

Tomek woke up in the middle of the night. He'd just had a dream, and Marie was saying to him, with a big smile full of confidence: 'Do you want to try to leave the island, Tomek? I thought as much. Since I saw you were prepared to cross the forest all by yourself, I knew you were a courageous boy capable of anything. I am sure you will succeed . . .'

It was barely daybreak. Everyone on the island was still asleep. Tomek reckoned that the biggest danger was certainly that of growing used to being there. A few days might be enough to accept the idea of staying, and a few weeks to become fully resigned to it. Especially if the island was as good a place to live as Tolgom claimed. No, he definitely must not wait. Or think about it.

Tomek got dressed without a sound and tiptoed out of the house. On the beach, he found a fishing boat, jumped into it and started rowing out to sea. On his bed he'd left just a brief note.

Dear Mr Bastibalagom,
 I'm going to try and sail under the black rainbow. If I don't come back, keep this bear knife as a memento of me, and try to live happily on the Island-That-Isn't.
 Tomek

He had taken only the little bottle of perfume that Pepigom had given him, and of course the pouch around his neck containing Hannah's coin. He told himself that it was probably his lucky charm, because, after all, he hadn't done too badly so far. The island gradually receded in the pink light of dawn, and when Tomek turned around, he saw the rainbow on the horizon. As Tolgom had described, it was no different from the one they had seen the day before. Just as brilliant, just as majestic. Tomek rowed for a good twenty minutes or so before the colours began to fade. There was still time to change his mind. Nothing was stopping him.

Turn back, Tomek, a voice inside him said. *Go back to the port and put this boat back where you found it, go home to Tolgom, snuggle up in your warm bed and don't tell anyone about your crazy venture.*

But his arms continued rowing and he stayed on course. 'Oh Lord, please help me,' he groaned when the rainbow turned a muddy grey and then black. It was even more terrifying than he had imagined. He stopped rowing and let the boat drift for a few seconds. The water became still and black, like that of a dead lake. He dipped his fingers in. It was freezing. The thought of diving into it was unbearable. A greyish mist rose. He waited in the silence, and just when he was about to continue rowing towards the rainbow, he heard a rhythmic creaking. It sounded like a wheelbarrow in need of a drop of oil, or rather a . . . Tomek *recognised* that sound, but he couldn't name it. All of a sudden, he was able to make out a shape moving above him and he knew immediately what it was: *a swing . . .*

Suspended from the rainbow was a giant swing whose iron hooks squeaked horribly. The only sound to be heard was the regular squeaking of the swing in the mist. All life had stopped. Tomek wondered whether his own blood was still flowing. He shivered because a damp cold had descended over the water. He was tempted to row, to warm himself up a little, but the boat didn't move forward an inch. It was just then that he saw a creature sitting on the swing. He had never imagined such a hideous being could exist. The woman must have been more than a hundred and fifty years old. She was extremely thin – her arms and legs were nothing but bones with flabby strips of milky skin hanging from them.

'Hello, boy,' she croaked, her wild eyes boring into Tomek. 'Have you come to answer the question?'

What question? wondered Tomek, but he was speechless.

The old woman thrust out her skinny legs to make the swing go higher. She was completely naked except for a pair of white socks and girl's shoes on her feet. Her long, bony fingers seemed to have been gripping the ropes for so long that her black nails were embedded in her wrists and poking through them. She smiled as she swayed to and fro, but she never took her eagle eyes off Tomek.

'I'm going to ask you the question I asked the others,' she went on. 'And like the others, you won't be able to answer it, Tomek. You see, I know your name, and you'll soon be joining those who've drowned before you, your white belly bloated like theirs, at the very, very, very, *very* bottom of the ocean. Think carefully about it,

Tomek: the water is dark and freezing and you will sink slowly, slowly, slowly, *slowly*, Tomek, my angel, my poppet, my little sunshine, my—'

'Shut up!' yelled Tomek. 'You have no right to say that! Shut *up*!'

How could this witch know that that was what Tomek's mother had called him when he was a tiny child: my little sunshine, my poppet . . . ? He'd forgotten it himself, but now that she was saying those words, it all came back to him and he couldn't bear it.

'Mama!' he shouted. 'Help!'

And as the old woman guffawed at his misery, he yelled again and again: 'Shut up! Shut up! *Shut up!*'

Then calm and silence were restored. Again the only sound was the regular squeaking of the swing. The old lady was in no hurry to get it over with, so it seemed.

'What if I answer the question?' asked Tomek eventually.

The swing stopped in mid-air, at an impossible oblique angle, and the old woman whispered, 'If you answer it correctly, my sunshine, you will pass under the black rainbow. You will be the first, and after you, everyone will be able to pass as they please, and I will vanish for ever . . . That is what will happen if you answer correctly. But if you don't, my poppet . . .'

'Go ahead,' said Tomek, trembling with fear and with cold. 'Ask me.'

The old woman kicked the swing into motion again, flew back and forth a dozen times and froze once more. In a strange, metallic voice, she said: '*We are sisters, as delicate as the wings of a butterfly, but we can make the world disappear. Who are we?*'

There was a long silence. The old woman remained suspended in mid-air.

'Would you like me to repeat the question, little sunshine?'

'No,' snapped Tomek, who had heard perfectly well.

'Then I'm going to swing back and forth fifty times while you think of the answer . . .'

Then she thrust out her legs and the squeaking began again.

'*We are sisters . . . as delicate . . .*' murmured Tomek, but his mind was blank.

His thoughts drifted, randomly, making no sense.

'Will it bother you if I sing?' sniggered the witch, and without waiting for a reply, she started humming nursery rhymes.

She seemed to know every verse that had frightened Tomek when he was little, or that had made him laugh. She knew everything about him.

'*We are sisters . . . we can make the world disappear . . .*' repeated Tomek over and over again.

Gradually he began to despair.

'Twenty-two . . . twenty-three . . .' croaked the witch.

Just then, Tomek felt the boat rock beneath him, or rather sink down slightly into the water. Enraged, he wanted to grab the oars and throw them in the old crone's face, but it was if they were welded to the boat and he couldn't lift them. He kept trying frantically, but to no avail.

'Well, my little sunshine, are you angry?' grimaced the witch.

Then the dark, freezing water began to seep into the boat and weigh it down. Tomek tried to scoop it out with his hands, but it was a waste of effort.

'Forty-eight, little sunshine, forty-eight and a half . . .'

Tomek knew then that it was over, that he was going to be swallowed up like the others, that he had to accept it. He wouldn't shout for help. He would not beg this hideous creature. He would just close his eyes so as not to see her any longer . . . to make her disappear . . . *disappear* . . . He jumped so violently that he nearly fell into the water. He knew at once that he'd found the answer! That the answer had just been given to him. That was it, of course! You just had to close your eyes . . . your *two* eyelids, eyelid *sisters*! *As delicate as butterfly wings* . . . and the whole world would disappear!

The water was up to his chest when he yelled with all his remaining strength: 'EYELIDS! EYELIDS!!!'

The witch froze at once. Tomek expected her to

howl and spit, but no, on the contrary, she was quiet. Her face was peaceful, and her eyes slowly closed. Then, within a few seconds, she completed her transformation and soon all that could be seen on the swing was the graceful body of a little girl in a light dress.

'On a swing we will fly . . . over the rainbow sky . . .' sang the little girl, thrusting her legs forward.

The water had turned blue again and was lapping around the boat. The rainbow grew pale and gradually regained its colours. Meanwhile, the little girl was swinging so high that her feet seemed to touch the sky. Finally, with a peal of laughter, she took off from the swing and flew off with the grace of a bird.

Tomek seized the oars and dipped them in the water. This time that boat responded perfectly. Tomek rowed manically.

'I did it! I did it!' he shouted at the top of his voice.

Above his head was a cascade of colours. A thousand harps played for him. In the distance, the little Island-That-Isn't was just beginning to stir.

CHAPTER FIFTEEN

The Cliff

Tomek's feat caused considerable astonishment then excitement. For as long as they had been deprived of their freedom, the island's inhabitants had been resigned to their fate. But now they had this freedom, now it had miraculously been restored to them, each person admitted that all the time they had secretly hoped for it and dreamed about it at night, and that their dearest wish was to be able to leave the island some day before they died. Tomek was hugged more in two days that he had been in his entire life.

The witch's riddle was on everyone's lips. 'Easy-peasy!' said the children. 'I could have found that!' But the adults knew very well that if no one had managed to solve the conundrum, it was because of the terror that numbed people's minds and stopped them from thinking straight. It had taken Tomek's youthful courage to overcome it.

The *Valiant* sailed from the Island-That-Isn't five

days later. On board were Captain Bastibalagom, his fourteen sailors, Tomek, and two young men who didn't have the patience to wait any longer. The fact was that the other ships moored alongside each other in the harbour weren't yet ready to put to sea. So it was decided that on its return, the *Valiant* would stop off at the Island-That-Isn't and that all the other ships would sail in procession behind it until they reached the land of the perfume makers. And so the island's inhabitants would have to wait a good two months before setting sail.

The *Valiant*'s voyage was without incident. The winds were favourable, and, naturally, the mood on board was exuberant. A big storm blew up during the second week, but Bastibalagom, who was a seasoned sailor, took it in his stride and no damage was done. They even spotted the black flag of a pirate ship a few days later, and the captain had a hard job calming the sailors who wanted to attack them and give that band of buffoons 'a memorable thrashing' once and for all. They had bonded so closely as a result of the ordeals they'd been through together that they were no longer afraid of anyone or anything.

'Please, gentlemen,' admonished Bastibalagom, 'we're not a battleship! We sell perfumes!'

And he steered the *Valiant* away from them.

As they drew closer to the continent, Tomek felt an anxiety he hadn't experienced for months: he would soon have to say goodbye to his perfume-maker friends and continue his journey alone. Each time this thought got him down, he sniffed the scent Pepigom had given him, and then Hannah was there, as if she were sitting next to him. *Where is she now?* he wondered. *Will I ever see her again?* He wanted the voyage to end quickly.

'Land ahoy!' cried the lookout one fine morning, and the sailors, who had now had enough of the sight of the sea, responded with a jubilant 'Hooray!'

Tomek helped unload the crates of perfume and the supplies. Three sailors would stay on board the ship to keep watch over it. The others and their captain would head east, where the population was scattered about. As for Tomek, he would set off westward where there wasn't a living soul, according to Bastibalagom, but it was probably where the River Qjar was. How far away was it? How many days would it take to walk to it? Weeks? No one could say. Tomek simply hoped that he would have time to reach it and get back before the perfume makers set sail again.

'One month,' Bastibalagom had said. 'We'll put to sea in one month. We might wait one day longer for you if you're not there, but no more.'

'Of course,' Tomek had replied. 'I understand . . .'

And now they had to part company for good. They gave him a bag of food that should be enough for four days at least. Then each of the sailors embraced him.

Bastibalagom was the last, and he pressed Tomek to his chest for a long time.

'Good luck, my son . . .' he said at length, gently nudging him onto the path heading westwards.

Tomek walked with a heavy heart for two or three minutes, then he turned around. None of the sailors had budged. They all watched him set out. They raised their arms to wave one last time, and he waved back.

'See you soon!' he shouted as loudly as he could, but the wind was against him and they couldn't hear him.

The path gradually wound its way up to the top of a steep cliff. From there, the view was magnificent: to the right, the ocean, more green than blue, and to the left, a moor dotted with shrubs and rocks. Tomek hiked for a good part of the day without feeling tired, stopping only to eat and drink. When night fell, he wrapped himself in his blanket and went to sleep under the shelter of a big rock, while the ocean waves roared close by.

The next day was exactly the same as the first, as was the day after that, and Tomek was unsure whether he'd been walking for three days or four. No matter how hard he'd tried to keep track, he'd lost count. The rocks all looked alike, the moor was endless, the wind blew relentlessly, and one morning it was so strong that Tomek had to stay in the shelter of his rock, unable to leave. But the most worrying thing was his bag of provisions was getting lighter and lighter . . .

One evening, he saw a pod of whales playing close to the shore. They were diving repeatedly, striking the water with their enormous tails. Tomek watched them for a long time, sitting in the tall grass and munching the last biscuit given to him by the perfume makers. His waterskin was nearly empty too. *If I don't arrive somewhere tomorrow, things are likely to go very badly for me . . .*

The following day, he had to set off on an empty stomach. By mid-morning, he could feel his legs giving way under him and he had to sit down for a moment. *What shall I do?* he pondered. *If I go further inland, I won't find anything more than here, and I'll risk getting lost.*

He tried to have a good rest and then continue on his way. Shortly afterwards, the wind seemed to be calming down a little, and the sky changed its hue. He barely had time to think about it when, all of a sudden, the space in front of him opened up to reveal a completely different landscape.

The cliff led down to a beach of pale yellow sand, and beyond this beach stretched a forest of tall, green trees, as far as the eye could see. Tomek ran down in spite of his wobbly legs. Once at the foot, he realised that the trees were laden with fruits he had never seen before. To start with, he picked a sort of giant apricot as heavy as a melon. When he split it open, a milk-like juice poured out. He drank cautiously at first, and then thirstily. It tasted a little like almond milk. Then, using his fingernail, he dug out a little of the tender flesh. It was delicious. Then he relished some string beans that tasted of liquorice, and strange soft cake-fruits as scrumptious as gingerbread. But his best discovery was some blackish balls with a very tough shell, full of a warm, creamy mash that tasted comfortingly of boiled potatoes. Sitting on a rock, Tomek ate his fill, sometimes drinking from his giant apricot.

He was about to stand up and set off again, when an ant clambered onto his hand. Instead of brushing it away, Tomek examined it carefully. It looked like any other ant, but with one big difference: it moved backwards . . . That was a tiny detail, of course, but it bothered Tomek and old Isham's words came back to him: '*There are species of animals that are completely unknown elsewhere,*' he'd said. Tomek blew the little insect off his hand and continued on his way.

Isham hadn't been lying, and what Tomek discovered in the following hours was beyond the imagination.

The creatures he met were so strange that he couldn't even name them. All he could say was what they were like . . . or what they reminded him of . . . An almost entirely flat animal, a sort of crawling dinner plate, came up close to Tomek, gazed at him wistfully for a few seconds, then waved a little bell that served as its tail before moving off again. A little later, a dozen huge birds cast their shadows on the ground. They had no wings, but a sort of broad, webbed tail like a mermaid's, with which they slowly fanned the air behind them. *They're swimming in the air!* Tomek said inwardly, and that was exactly right. They had no beaks either, but little snub noses that made them look like rabbits with moustaches. But Tomek hadn't yet seen the most weird and wonderful thing of all – little rodents that slept curled up in a ball. At first he'd mistaken these for an unknown fruit, but now the squirrel-like creatures were awake and swinging from the ends of the supple branches in a graceful overhead ballet. Tomek thought they were just ordinary squirrels but, on looking more closely, he realised the incredible truth: each one was *part* of the branch, an extension of it, and had grown there like a living fruit, an animal-fruit . . . In fact, the tree was full of dozens of similar creatures. How on earth could they feed themselves, mused Tomek, but he had no time to think about it any longer: a barely audible, far-off noise came to his ears. It sounded like running water. He hastened his steps, his heart pounding. Had he finally arrived? After so much effort, so many hopes? The forest was thinning out and he ran through the few remaining trees, climbed one last hill and stood rooted to the spot in amazement.

There was a river flowing tranquilly in front of his eyes. In the distance, to the right, you could see the ocean it had come from, and to the left, on the horizon, the foothills towards which it was silently wending its way.

'The River Qjar . . .' murmured Tomek, overwhelmed. 'The River Qjar . . . I've found it . . .'

CHAPTER SIXTEEN

The River

Tomek spent the last hours of daylight making a raft. He found everything he needed at his fingertips: plenty of tree trunks, vines to bind them together, sharp stones to cut the vines. He greatly enjoyed the work, and within a few hours the raft was finished, without Tomek feeling too tired. There'd been just one scary moment when he began to break off a long branch to make a pole: there was a squirrel-fruit at the end of it. When Tomek apologised, the little animal shook its head from right to left as if to say: *Are you out of your mind?* And it was such a funny sight that Tomek burst out laughing. Every so often, he stopped for a little rest, and then he couldn't help going to dip his hands in the river and letting the water run through his fingers. He wanted to drink some, but it was still salty. It would probably be less so higher up, he told himself.

Dusk was already falling, so he decided not to set off that night, and he lay down to sleep under a big tree, nice and snug in his blanket. It was good not to hear the rumble of the ocean any more. He felt lovely and warm and cosy. He was just falling asleep when he heard a deep sigh. He opened his eyes and saw that the branches of the trees around him were slowly drooping until they almost touched the ground. *Trees that let out sighs* . . . he recalled with a smile. Just as Isham had said. The tree under which he had bedded down wasn't sighing, but just above Tomek's head, two squirrel-fruits had come together and were slowly dozing off, clutching each other. He could see their eyelids close, open and close again.

'Good night!' whispered Tomek, and he too drifted off to sleep.

He was woken by the sun. The trees around him had raised their branches and were stretching, all trying to outdo one another. It was fun to watch and made him feel like doing the same. Overhead, the two little squirrel-fruits were stretching too, and Tomek joined in.

After breakfasting on various fruits and a little apricot milk, he began to load his raft. He took a dozen of the big nuts full of yummy mashed potato. That would make a good meal when he felt hungry. He also took with him several giant apricots for their milk. And finally, he made a fairly solid paddle from a length of bark, jumped onto the raft and pushed off from the shore aided by his pole. The little craft spun around twice before righting itself in the centre of the river, then it was picked up by the current.

It is hard to imagine anything more tranquil. 'If there is a heaven,' Tomek said to himself, 'then it must be something like this . . .' Small, brightly coloured parrots perched fearlessly on the raft to peck at the fruits. Tomek tried to shoo them off, but they kept coming back and he gave up and let them come and go. He was escorted all afternoon by manatees whose eyes looked so intelligent that he wanted to talk to them. The day went by uneventfully, with nothing disturbing the utter tranquillity. That night, Tomek camped on the shore and at dawn he continued his calm voyage.

Towards the late morning, he saw far ahead of him a glistening wall damming the river. A waterfall, he realised as he drew closer. Only this water didn't 'fall'. Quite the opposite, it rose, serenely, without any foam, in a perfect upward sweep. *What a miracle!* thought Tomek, remembering the waterfall back home, so noisy and bubbling, so full of fury. But this one reminded him of a supple, silent animal, a black panther . . . He grabbed his oar and tried to row to the shore, but he didn't make it in time and ran into the waterfall. The front of the raft rose up vertically. For a moment, Tomek had the wonderful feeling that he was going to defy gravity and that the current would carry him up into the air, right to the top, maybe. But no, he barely had time to grab his blanket and a few nuts, when everything turned upside-down. He swam easily to a flat rock on the shore. There, he took off all his clothes and laid them out to dry on the surface. Since he had nothing else to do but wait, he dived into the clear water and swam to the upside-down waterfall. It was a fascinating game. He allowed himself to be tossed up fifteen feet by the current, then he plunged downwards in freefall, laughing and shrieking as if drunk, and his naked body made a deafening splash in the vast silence of the river, giving the fish a fright. This place was probably the same as it had been millions of years ago, he mused. How many human beings had swum in this water before him? There was something eternal about it. Exhausted from physical effort and happiness, he finally lay down on the rock and abandoned himself to the sun's gentle caress.

By mid-afternoon, his clothes were dry. He was about to set off again when he had the impression that in the far distance, where the river disappeared among the trees, a darker shadow was dancing on the water. He waited a while and soon he was certain that a small boat was heading towards him. A raft like his, perhaps. And there were people sitting on it. The last living people Tomek had seen were the perfume makers, and that had been more than five days ago. His heart started racing. Who were these people? Friends? Foes? He took his bear knife from his pocket and opened it.

But as the raft became more visible, Tomek's heart missed a beat. And it wasn't through fear. Because without seeing her, without actually recognising her, he was certain it was her: Hannah. That graceful form was *her*, he was absolutely convinced. But then who was the second person, half hidden behind her? Who did that massive body belong to? Never had Tomek imagined seeing Hannah again other than alone. And now this long-awaited moment had come, here she was with someone else . . .

When they drew near, Hannah stood up on the raft and froze. She had probably recognised Tomek, but she wasn't completely certain yet. When she was, she launched into a sort of joyful caper, waved her arms above her head and yelled: 'Mr Grocer! It's me! It's me!'

'Hannah! It's me,' replied Tomek. Then he added at once: 'Wait! Have you got an oar? Row over here!'

He didn't want Hannah to do what he had done and fall into the water with her friend. But she didn't seem the least bothered by the danger. Instead, she took a running jump and threw herself into the water before the raft reached the upside-down waterfall. She swam like a fish and the minute she was out of the water she flung herself around Tomek's neck and kissed him.

'What's your name?'

'Tomek,' replied Tomek, stunned by her easy familiarity.

'Tomek? Good, because that's a lovely name,' said Hannah. 'Better than Glupot in any case!' she added, bursting out laughing.

Then she turned to her companion, who was crouching on the edge of the raft and didn't dare jump.

'Glupot! There's nothing to be afraid of! Dive in and swim over here!' she shouted at him, and then said in a hushed voice to Tomek: 'He's a bit of scaredy-cat and he hates getting his fur wet . . .'

Only then did Tomek realise that Glupot wasn't a human being but an animal. What sort? It was hard to say.

'Is he . . . a bear?' he ventured, partially reassured.

'No, not really,' replied Hannah. 'Rather a sort of panda, I think. He doesn't have claws or fangs and he only eats leaves.'

Meanwhile, Glupot had toppled into the water and then laboriously splashed his way over to the rocks. When he emerged, he seemed to have lost half his bulk, and Hannah found him hilarious.

'Glupot, go and shake yourself over there, please!' she admonished him.

But it was too late and Tomek was already soaked to the skin.

'How ill-mannered!' complained Hannah. 'He knows he can get away with anything because of his cute looks, so he does as he pleases. Say hello, Glupot!'

Glupot, who was now standing on his hind legs like a human, gazed woefully at Tomek and . . . held out his paw. It was true that he had a sweet face. Tomek looked from the panda to Hannah, then from Hannah to the panda. He had imagined all sorts of possible reunions with the barley-sugar girl, but he hadn't for one moment thought that they would meet up again under the rueful gaze of giant panda who would proffer his paw. *Life is more inventive than I am*, he mused. And he shook Glupot's paw.

Tomek and Hannah had so much to tell each other that they didn't know where to begin. They had a thousand questions on their lips, and it was impossible to answer them all at once.

'When you were in the Forest of Oblivion . . .' began Tomek.

'The Forest of what?' said Hannah.

Tomek had to explain it to her. She had crossed it without knowing! On the other hand, the spine-chilling scream that Tomek and Marie had heard was definitely her.

'I was perched on a branch, scared out of my wits, and this idiotic bear just beneath me was waiting for me to make the slightest sound to gobble me up. After keeping quiet for an hour, I'd had enough. I said to myself: Do you want to hear something? Well, you're going to *hear* something! And I jumped into his ear. Just imagine, it was big enough to hold all of me! All of me inside a bear's ear! And I screamed as loudly as I could. At the top of my lungs! I can scream very loudly, you know . . . Do you want to hear?'

'No, there's no need, I believe you . . .' said Tomek.

'Then the bear went crazy. I think I gave him a burst eardrum. Then I tumbled out of his ear and ran straight ahead. I was lucky I chose the right direction . . . do you know Pepigom?'

'Um, yes . . .' said Tomek. 'She's very kind. Do you know her well too?'

They chatted nineteen to the dozen, getting everything muddled up, so keen were they to tell each other about their adventures. They talked about the little perfume makers, the meadow, the big blue flowers called sails, the forest with squirrel-fruits . . .

'That's where I met Glupot,' said Hannah. 'I was asleep under a tree and at dawn, at the hour where you usually feel the cold, I was surprised to be so warm and snug. I have a woollen blanket, but all the same . . . Then I heard snoring a few inches from my face. I opened my eyes. It was Glupot. You'll soon understand why I called him that! In any case, I recommend him at night. There's nothing more comfortable. He's a pillow, eiderdown *and* hot-water bottle all in one, and besides that he's so calm that lying next to him, you fall asleep within seconds.'

Hannah hadn't come across the cliff – because she

had come via a completely different route, which was much longer in fact – or of course the Island-That-Isn't, because she'd crossed the ocean on another boat from a different starting point. Tomek told her about his voyage, and he also asked her the witch's riddle. Hannah answered without hesitation and immediately apologised, sensing he was a little annoyed . . .

When they were tired from talking so much, their clothes were dry, and the afternoon was drawing to a close. Glupot woke up from his nap and came and snuggled up to Hannah, hoping she'd stroke him.

'You see! He's so cuddly!'

Tomek wondered if it was possible to be jealous of a panda called Glupot.

Clambering up the rocks beside the waterfall was child's play. At the top, a surprise awaited them: the vegetation was sparser and the river was more like a wide stream. A few hundred yards away, there was a bend. They headed towards it and as soon as they rounded it, they saw what Tomek had been eager to find for so long: a steep mountain rose up before them. The last rays of the setting sun illuminated its summit. The mountain appeared to touch the sky.

'It's so beautiful!' breathed Hannah. 'It's like a cathedral!'

'Yes,' said Tomek, 'it's the Sacred Mountain. The river stops up at the top.'

'Shall we go?' asked Hannah excitedly.

'Let's,' replied Tomek.

Only Glupot seemed a little reluctant. Hiking wasn't his strong point. All three kept going as far as they could along the riverbank. The path grew steeper and steeper. Before nightfall, they set up camp behind a big rock. Hannah had a firesteel and they made a fire. They each ate one of the big nuts that Tomek had brought, then snuggled up together.

Before falling asleep, Tomek recalled old Isham's words: *'No one, and I mean* no one, *has ever returned with the tiniest drop of this famous water . . . that's as impossible as getting corn to grow on the back of my hand . . .'* He gazed at the Sacred Mountain which was now a huge, dark, threatening mass towering over them, and he shuddered. He was no longer alone, but strangely, he didn't find that at all comforting, quite the opposite. *I'm the eldest*, he thought. *I must protect her . . .* And he snuggled up in his blanket and against Glupot's warm fur.

'Tell me, Tomek,' murmured Hannah sleepily, 'what's in that little pouch around your neck?'

Without answering, he opened the pouch, took out the coin and slipped it into Hannah's hand.

'Here, it's the coin you gave me when you came into my shop. I'm returning it to you.'

'Oh, thank you, that's so kind of you . . .' was all she could stammer.

'Good night, Hannah,' he said again.

And since she was already asleep, he added: 'Good night to you too, Glupot . . .'

And the great beast gave a gentle grunt that probably meant 'Good night' in panda language.

CHAPTER SEVENTEEN

The Sacred Mountain

At dawn, the mountain didn't look as menacing as it had done the previous day. Instead, it seemed to be inviting them to climb it. The three travellers ate the last of their provisions, then they set off in a light-hearted mood. There was no doubt that they would be back that same evening with their two waterskins filled from the River Qjar. Or so they thought. The water was no longer salty but crystal clear. It was a constant source of amazement to see it flowing backwards, leaping over rocks and splashing them with its foam. Even though Tomek and Hannah had become used to this phenomenon since the ocean, they couldn't help stopping from time to time to gaze at it, their hands on their hips.

'It's incredible, isn't it?' one would say.

And the other would reply: 'Yes, it's absolutely amazing . . .'

Then they'd continue their climb. Glupot was

struggling more and more to heave his plump body towards the summit. He was huffing and puffing like a steam engine and, around midday, he even plonked himself down on a rock with the stubborn expression of someone who refuses to walk another step. Hannah had to take his paw and plead with him: 'Come on, Glupot! You can do it! The exercise will do you good. And we can't just leave you here all by yourself!'

Tomek and Hannah began to wonder whether they had done the right thing in bringing him with them on the climb, but they would soon change their minds because the giant panda saved them from a nasty predicament.

All of a sudden, in the middle of the afternoon, Hannah, who was walking in front, gave a little shriek.

'Oh! Tomek, look! The stream's disappearing underground!'

And so it was. At this point, the stream was only about eighteen inches wide, and it ran straight into the mountain. The three adventurers stood stock still.

'It doesn't matter,' said Tomek after a while, a little disconcerted. 'We'll keep going up, and I'll bet you anything you like we'll come across it again a little higher.'

But sadly, after more than two hours' of seeking, of toing and froing, going up and down, they had to admit that they had well and truly lost the River Qjar. They even had great difficulty in finding their way back to the spot where it had entered the mountain. They came across it eventually, and they sat down, feeling lost, and wondering what was going to become of them. That was when Glupot came and nuzzled the side of Hannah's dress.

'I know what you want, you greedy thing!' she said fondly. 'Here! But look, it's the last one . . .'

And she took from her pocket one of those liquorice-flavoured beans that he loved to suck. She was about to give it to him when Tomek stopped her: 'Wait, Hannah! I have an idea. It's probably crazy but at this point . . . Tell me, do pandas have a good sense of smell?'

'I have no idea . . .' replied Hannah, baffled. 'Perhaps they do.'

Then Tomek snatched the bean and made Glupot sniff it.

'You heard, Glupot: it's the last one. Hannah hasn't got any more. Do you understand? Well, look what I'm doing with the last one . . .'

And he threw it into the stream. The little bean disappeared at once, swept away by the current. Glupot was a stranger to anger, he wasn't capable of it, but on seeing his treat float away, he began to moan and whimper like a miserable child. Tomek put his arm around his neck.

'Listen to me, Glupot . . . your bean isn't lost . . . it's going to follow the stream underground and come out

again up there ... do you understand? Glupot ...
Please ... *bean* ... *up there* ...'

And he pointed up to the top of the mountain.
Glupot looked at him with tear-filled eyes, then he
suddenly grasped what Tomek was saying, and they had
to move very fast to keep up with him. He began to trot,
his muzzle to the ground, sniffing, grunting. Tomek and
Hannah barely had time to gather their belongings, and
already they were running as fast as their legs could carry
them behind Glupot who no longer even looked round
at them. They were off on a mad dash through the rocks.

'Tired, my foot!' shouted Tomek. 'He really took us
for a ride back there!'

'Glupot, wait for us!' Hannah called out, laughing.
'Not so fast!'

In spite of their efforts, Tomek and Hannah were
soon left behind and they found themselves alone in the
vast silence of the mountain. They were beginning to
wonder whether they had now lost both the river and
the panda, when they saw Glupot reappear in the
distance, jumping up and down in delight and waving at
them. As soon as they drew nearer, they could see the
bean, which he was holding in his mouth like a cigarette.
Between his paws the River Qjar was flowing backwards.
Now it was no more than a thin trickle, as narrow as a
child's wrist.

'Well done, Glupot! Well done!' whooped Hannah,

and she threw herself at his neck with such force that he toppled over backwards.

The two of them play-fought, rolling on the ground and knocking each other over in turn, laughing and shrieking.

'And well done to you too, Tomek,' said Hannah breathlessly after a while, and she kissed him on the cheek.

They sat there for a moment, thrilled at having found their way again. They drank thirstily too and found that the water was increasingly light and crystalline.

They walked on for a good hour, praying that the trickle of water wouldn't vanish underground again, but nothing of the sort happened and once again it was nightfall that forced them to stop.

'Are you hungry?' asked Hannah, as the sun's dying rays played on the mountain peaks.

'No, it's odd, but I'm not hungry,' replied Tomek. 'It's as if the water satisfied me. And I'm not tired, either. What about you, are you hungry?'

It was the same for Hannah. She felt fine and didn't want to eat. When the evening turned cool, they both snuggled up to Glupot and held hands. Before falling asleep completely, Tomek gazed at the huge shadows of the clouds on the mountainside and felt the same anxiety as the day before. *So where is the danger?* he wondered. *Why has no one ever been able to bring back some of this water?*

Close to his ear, the brook murmured: 'You'll soon find out, Tomek, you'll soon find out . . .'

The next day, they spoke little. They were content to walk in silence. Most of the time, Tomek walked in front. Hannah followed him, sometimes holding Glupot's hand. The big panda didn't complain. He too seemed to have drawn new strength from the water. Gradually, the vegetation grew thinner. There wasn't a breath of wind, either. As if time were standing still. The only sign of life was the cheerful babble of the brook. By late afternoon, the climb suddenly grew steeper, and they had to claw their way up using their arms and hands.

'I do believe,' said Tomek turning around, 'that we've reached the top . . .'

They clambered up the last few feet without losing sight of the trickle of water that was now the thickness of a thumb. Tomek had not been mistaken. They soon reached a flat area a few yards wide and realised that they were at the summit. The sight that greeted them took their breath away. From this point, they had a view over a fairy-tale landscape. Hundreds and hundreds of mountains with snow-covered peaks rose up around them. But the one they were on was the highest. It felt as if they were on the roof of the world. Tomek wanted to say something to Hannah, but on turning around, he saw that she was on her knees. He went over to her. At his feet, the River Qjar's thin trickle of water ended in the hollow of a rock. He kneeled down beside her.

'It's empty ... there's nothing ...' whispered Hannah, on the verge of tears.

It was true. There was nothing in the hollow. Tomek was so flabbergasted that at first, he was numbed. What most upset him was seeing Hannah's distress.

'All that for nothing,' she said in a broken voice. 'The endless journey, the suffering ... We have gone to such great pains, Tomek ...'

Not knowing how to console her, he picked up a little stone and idly threw it into the hollow. Then they heard a soft 'plink' and they saw the water tremble and form a few little ripples. The stone basin wasn't empty at all! It was full of water, but it was so incredibly still, so wonderfully clear and light, that it was invisible. It was *intangible*. Tomek and Hannah plunged their trembling hands into it.

'The water that stops people from ever dying ...' said Hannah softy, and this time she really was crying.

She wept for a long time. Tomek knew she was thinking about her father: '*Which bird would you like, Hannah? Which one would please you?*' but he kept quiet. He himself was thinking about his parents; he said nothing about them either. Fat tears rolled down his cheeks.

They stayed silent for a long time, squeezing each other's hands in the water.

'Are you thirsty, Tomek?' asked Hannah finally, with a smile, and she looked up at him with her huge dark eyes.

'Yes,' replied Tomek. 'Are you?'

'Yes . . .'

But they did not drink. All of a sudden, they felt fragile in the face of something so immense and overwhelming. And the same serious questions were going through their young heads: Can a person really wish never to die . . . ?

Is it not precisely *because* life comes to an end one day that it is so precious . . . ?

Isn't the idea of living for ever even more frightening than that of dying . . . ?

And if you never die, then when will you be reunited with your loved ones who have already passed away . . . ?

Tomek knew at once that he would not drink. All the same he cupped some water in the palms of his hands, for the pleasure of holding it. But the water didn't stay there. It ran through his fingers onto the rock. He tried a second time, but with no more success. The water ran out through all the cracks, climbed the wall made by his fingers, impossible to capture. *As impossible as growing corn on the back of his hand* . . . so *that* was it! Only that. This water did indeed exist, but no one could take it . . .

Hannah had watched without saying anything.

'Let me try . . .'

She made a small round bowl with her delicate fingers and captured a tiny amount of water, then, with infinite care, she raised it, but exactly the same thing happened as with Tomek: the water overflowed and drained away.

'You see . . . It's impossible,' sighed Tomek.

'Wait,' breathed Hannah, all of a sudden. 'Look!'

A single drop remained in the palm of her hand, as round and delicate as a pearl.

'Look . . . I'm allowed to take one drop, no more. I imagine it's for my little songbird . . .'

Her face lit up with joy. She repeated the experiment over and over again, and each time, a single drop remained. Although Tomek never managed to keep any of the water, Hannah's delight made up for it.

'How are we going to take this drop away?' he asked after a while. 'We're not going to put it in a waterskin, are we?'

'I've got something better,' replied Hannah, impishly.

On her finger she wore a ring with a tiny hinged lid. She slid the drop in and it just filled the space inside. Then she closed the lid.

'Perfect . . . If it's still there tomorrow morning, there's no reason why it won't stay.'

Just then, the first stars appeared in the sky, then

hundreds of others. Tomek had never seen such a bright sky. They lay down to admire the Milky Way. They were no longer on Earth, gazing at the stars. They were among the stars, surrounded by them. They were minuscule parts of the infinite cosmos.

The night cold made them shiver, so Glupot, who for once had kept his distance, came over to Hannah and Tomek and gave them his warmth.

CHAPTER EIGHTEEN

The Return

Tomek and Hannah took a long time to get back to the ocean from the Sacred Mountain because they couldn't sail down the river on a raft as they had done on the way there.

They said goodbye to their kind friend Glupot one morning under a squirrel-fruit tree where they'd spent the night. While the big panda was asleep, they silently gathered their belongings and left without him. It was heartbreaking for Hannah, of course, but it was best for everyone. Glupot would have been too unhappy far from his trees and his liquorice-flavoured beans.

Then they walked as fast as they could along the cliff, constantly wondering whether they would return too late and whether the *Valiant* would already have set sail. So it was a great joy when, one fine morning, they saw a horse and cart coming towards them driven by Bastibalagom himself. The good captain had not only waited an extra day as promised, but here he was coming to meet them and help them! He hugged Hannah and Tomek to him as if they were his own children. What's more, he hadn't at all expected to see Hannah, and that brought tears to his eyes.

The *Valiant* sailed without incident to the Island-That-Is, as it was now called, Bastibalagom told them. On the Island-That-Is, Tomek and Hannah were able to rest after their ordeals of the past few weeks, then they boarded the ship again. But this time, the *Valiant* was at the head of the most incredible fleet ever seen on that ocean. Sixteen sailing ships, all-white sails hoisted, followed in its wake in a dazzling procession. The entire population of the Island-That-Is was on board.

When they arrived within sight of the land of the perfume makers, the other ships waited out at sea and let the *Valiant* sail into the harbour alone. The arrival of the entire fleet would have been too great a shock for the perfume makers, who hadn't been forewarned. They would have to be told, prepared for the incredible event they were about to experience, and so it was only the next day that the sixteen sailing ships put in to shore and all the inhabitants of the Island-That-Is disembarked. Heartrending scenes followed, as you can imagine. Because while the brave little perfume makers remained cheerful and smiling in sorrow and misfortune, on the other hand, they cried their eyes out when they were overcome with joy.

Pepigom did not feel at all sad on seeing Tomek and Hannah arm in arm because she had a fiancé too, as rotund, jolly and as kind as her. During the days that followed, there were scenes of jubilation. People ate lots of bacon pancakes, drank plenty of cider, danced and sang.

But one evening, Tomek told Hannah that he would like to leave, because he feared that if he waited any longer, he would miss Marie at the edge of the Forest of Oblivion, and he was anxious to see her again. So they left the next day, promising to return soon. Eztergom said again that both of them were like their own children and that they would always have a place in their hearts. He gave them each a pair of the little perfume makers' special noseplugs so they would have nothing to fear from the flowers in the meadow.

Once again, the journey was magical, and they walked at a brisk pace all morning. But around midday, Tomek stopped in his tracks and exclaimed: 'Hannah! We almost forgot something very important!'

So saying, he took from his pocket one of his two handkerchiefs embroidered with a 'T' for Tomek and tied a knot.

'What do you want to be reminded about?' asked Hannah.

'Well,' replied Tomek, 'I want to be reminded that there is something that I won't remember and that I mustn't forget . . .'

Hannah looked perplexed.

'Tomek, are you certain that your noseplugs are firmly in place? You haven't breathed in . . .'

'Not at all,' replied Tomek, laughing. 'It's very simple. Supposing that Marie is entering the Forest of Oblivion now, she'll be erased from our memories at once and so it won't occur to us to wait for her there . . . This knot means: *Someone will come. Wait for them!* Do you see?'

Hannah had to admit that his idea was very clever.

A little farther, as they were walking amid the huge flowers called sails, Tomek started to feel very frightened, and Hannah, who was a few yards ahead of him, suddenly began to sway and teeter.

'Your nostrils!' yelled Tomek. 'Pinch your nostrils!'

But her legs had already turned to jelly. She fell flat on her face onto the ground and closed her eyes. Tomek raced over and took her face in his hands.

'Hannah! Please, wake up!'

But now she was in a deep sleep. Tomek had a few spare noseplugs and he immediately put one in Hannah's empty nostril. Then he tried to concentrate. What were the Awakening Words for Hannah? Eztergom had told him, he was certain. The old man had even added that they had been easy to discover. All of a sudden, the words came back to him and he leaned over Hannah's ear and whispered lovingly, '*Once upon a time . . .*'

Hannah opened her eyes, yawned, then said with a smile, 'Tomek . . . you should have let me sleep . . . I was having such a lovely dream. You were in it.'

A few hours later, in the far distance, they saw a long dark ribbon stretching across the horizon. It was the Forest of Oblivion.

'Look,' said Hannah, when they reached the first trees. 'That appears to be a tomb . . .'

'It's Barnaby's grave,' replied Tomek. 'Barnaby was the . . .'

He wanted to say more, but he wasn't able to. Something was eluding him. He asked Hannah whether he'd told her about this Barnaby, by any chance. She said yes, he had told her, but she couldn't remember anything either. It was like a big gap in her mind.

They made a fire and ate the provisions they'd been given by the perfume makers. After their meal, as he was wiping his hands on his handkerchief, Tomek stopped abruptly.

'Look, Hannah . . . This knot . . .'

'Yes,' she recalled. 'It means that someone will be coming. Someone who is in the forest and who we must wait for . . .'

But no one came during the night, nor during the next day, and they were in the middle of their second supper in that spot when they heard a noise coming from the forest. It sounded like a cart driving along a path.

Then they heard a cheerful voice singing:

'Little donkey, little donkey
On the dusty road . . .'

Tomek's heart filled with such joy that he shouted 'Marie!' well before she emerged from the Forest of Oblivion.

The three of them talked late into the night by the fireside. Trotter, who was missing an ear by now, was asleep on his feet a little farther away.

They spent the following morning beside Barnaby's grave, and then they all set off across the Forest of Oblivion. The bears kept away this time, and the three travellers reached the other side without mishap.

Marie accompanied Tomek and Hannah for a few more miles, then their paths diverged, and they said their goodbyes. On seeing them walk off hand in hand, Marie simply shouted after them: 'Make the most of it, children!'

They walked at a good pace but weren't able to reach Tomek's village before nightfall. Once again, they had to sleep under the stars, and only arrived the next morning. First, they dropped in to see old Isham because he had the key to the grocery, and above all because Tomek was eager to see him. The old man was sitting cross-legged at his writing stand, as usual.

'Hello, Grandfather!' Tomek hailed from a distance. Hannah stayed back, not wanting to intrude on their reunion.

Isham watched Tomek come towards him, unable to believe his eyes, then, when he was absolutely certain he wasn't dreaming, he pressed his hands together in front of his face and said weakly: 'My son, my son . . . How big and strong you are. You were a child when you left and now you are a man! Let me embrace you . . .'

Tomek approached and knelt before him and clasped him for a long time. Then, breaking free, he brushed away his tears and said ruefully: 'Forgive me, Grandfather, but I wasn't able to bring back any water from the River Qjar for you . . . I . . .'

Isham smiled: 'Be comforted, my son, because I would not have drunk it. So don't be sorry. If I had the choice between a glass of that water and a piece of nougat, I would take the nougat! I don't *want* to live for ever, do you understand? I even think I shan't live much longer. I was eager to see you again. Now you are here, and that is enough. I don't ask anything more of life . . .'

'But, Grandfather, I need you! *I* want to keep you!'

'You want to keep me? Then I'll make a little effort just for you. But you see, Tomek, I am no longer any use.

My bones hurt. I would feel better in your memory than sitting in this draughty stall. And while we are on the subject, I'm going to tell you something. Listen carefully because I am only going to say this once . . . When I die, Tomek, cry a little if you can't help it, but not for too long, please. Perhaps you will come and visit my grave, every so often, but say to yourself that I will no longer be there. If you want to see me, you will have to turn around and look at the rows of trees in the wind, the puddle of water where the little bird is drinking, the puppy playing – *that's* where I will be Tomek. Never forget that. And now tell me who this pretty young lady hiding over there is . . . you haven't introduced us.'

An hour later, on pushing open the door of his grocery, Tomek was amazed. 'Goodness, it's so small . . .' he repeated more than ten times. 'It's so *small* . . .'

Meanwhile, Hannah remembered every drawer Tomek had opened a year earlier.

'In this one there are playing cards, here a picture of a kangaroo, and there, some desert sand in a tiny vial . . .'

She stayed for a few more days, and then one morning, she told Tomek that she was going to leave. She wanted to see her adoptive parents again and especially her little sister.

'Will you come back soon?' asked Tomek.

Seeing his woebegone expression, she slid the ring

containing the drop of water from her finger and gave it to him.

'Here, I'll leave this with you. That way you can be certain I'll return. I'm just going to fetch my little songbird. I'll be back very soon. I promise.'

And she was on her way.

EPILOGUE

Hannah returned less than three weeks later. It was morning and Tomek had just opened his shop. She pushed open the door, letting all the light from the street flood in. On her shoulder was perched the little songbird.

'Hannah!' cried Tomek, and his heart leaped for joy on seeing her again.

They chatted a little, then Tomek went to fetch the ring. Hannah snapped open the lid herself and rolled the drop into the palm of her hand. Then she picked up the bird in her other hand and placed her beside the waterdrop.

'Drink, please, my little bird, drink . . .' she said softly.

The songbird hesitated for a moment, then everything happened very fast: she bent towards the drop which glistened like a pearl, and slid it into her beak, and finally, she jerked her head back, tipping the water down her throat.

'There . . . She will never die . . .' murmured Hannah.

'No, she will never die,' echoed Tomek.

Then they placed the bird on a wooden perch that Tomek had built over the counter. Hannah watched her songbird for a long time in silence, then she said in a hushed voice: 'You know, Tomek, I've had the strangest thought . . .'

'What's that?' he asked.

'Well, just as the drop of water ran down her throat, I felt certain that the River Qjar started flowing the right way again . . . That it had only flowed backwards and upside down for this single drop of water, so that one day it would end up in the beak of this little songbird . . . and that it's all over now . . .'

Tomek listened, fascinated.

'You mean that what we saw on the mountain no longer exists?'

'I don't know . . . perhaps . . . It was all so strange . . .'

Tomek thought back to all the incredible things he had experienced: the Forest of Oblivion and its bears, the giant blue flowers called sails, the Island-That-Isn't that became the Island-That-Is, the witch on her swing, the squirrel-fruit trees . . .

'It's as if we'd dreamed it all . . .' continued Hannah. 'After all, we haven't brought anything else back from our journey. We've ended up empty-handed . . .'

Then a radiant smile lit up Tomek's face and he ran into the backroom. 'Oh yes we did, Hannah, *I* did, but there's one I haven't dared show you yet. Now the time has come, I think.'

And he held out the little bottle of perfume that Pepigom had concocted.

Hannah removed the stopper and took a deep breath. Then she saw the hill, the dancers and the musicians. She saw the bench on which she and Tomek were both seated, surrounded by their friends and beneath a shower of petals . . .

'Oh, Tomek . . .' she whispered.

'Are you going to stay for a while, this time?' asked Tomek, a lump in his throat.

'I'm going to stay for ever . . .' replied Hannah.

At that very moment, from her perch, the little bird whistled her first song of eternity.

Jefferson

JEAN-CLAUDE MOURLEVAT

TRANSLATED BY ROS SCHWARTZ

WINNER OF THE PEN TRANSLATES AWARD

**JEAN-CLAUDE MOURLEVAT IS THE 2021 WINNER
OF THE ASTRID LINDGREN MEMORIAL AWARD**

When Jefferson the hedgehog goes to his hairdresser's, he's
shocked to discover the barber lying dead on the floor. Falsely
accused of murder, Jefferson must go on the run with his best
friend Gilbert the pig to uncover the real killers. Adventure,
dark secrets and a most unlikely series of hair-raising events
await Jefferson and his fellow
animals as they travel into
the Land of the Humans . . .

'Charming and instructive,
fast-paced and entertaining –
but, most of all, these qualities
combine to deliver a powerful
message about the brutal
slaughter of animals for meat.
This is activism in soft but
deadly gloves' *Books for Keeps*

THE SNOW MERCHANT

SAM GAYTON

ILLUSTRATED BY CHRIS RIDDELL

Lettie Peppercorn lives in a house on stilts near the wind-swept coast of Albion. Nothing incredible has ever happened to her, until one winter's night.
The night the Snow Merchant comes.
He claims to be an alchemist – the greatest that ever lived – and in a mahogany suitcase, he carries his newest invention.
It is an invention that will change Lettie's life – and the world – forever. It is an invention called snow.

'A delightful debut . . . full of action and invention' *Sunday Times*

'A germ of JK and a pinch of Pullman' *TES*

9781783441778